Devil Mountain

Cades Cove Series
Book Three

by
Aiden James

BOOKS BY AIDEN JAMES

CADES COVE SERIES
Cades Cove
The Raven Mocker
Devil Mountain

DYING OF THE DARK VAMPIRES
With Patrick Burdine
The Vampires' Last Lover
The Vampires' Birthright
Blood Princesses

THE JUDAS CHRONICLES
Immortal Plague
Immortal Reign
Immortal Destiny
Immortal Dragon
Immortal Tyranny
Immortal Pyramid
Immortal Victory
Immortal Supremacy
Immortal Storm

NICK CAINE ADVENTURES
With J.R. Rain
Temple of the Jaguar
Treasure of the Deep
Pyramid of the Gods
Aiden James only
Curse of the Druids
Secret of the Loch
River of the Damned

Published 2019 by
Manor House Books

Cover Art: Michele Lee, Blue Sky Design ~
Boston

Printed in the United States of America.

Second Edition

CADES COVE SERIES: BOOK THREE

DEVIL MOUNTAIN

AIDEN JAMES

.

"Warriors are not what you think of as warriors. The warrior is not someone who fights, because no one has the right to take another life. The warrior, for us, is one who sacrifices himself for the good of others." ~ Sitting Bull

Devil Mountain

Prologue

June 30th.

Nearly six years have passed since trouble visited Cades Cove.

The events of that terrible time almost feel surreal now... or at least they did until very recently. I had hardly thought of Allie Mae McCormick and her quest for vengeance against my friend, David Hobbs, and his family for the crimes of his ancestor, Billy Ray Hobson. Her spirit now sleeps in peace.... Nor have I thought of the demon god, Teutates, believing he might not even be a true deity after his essence was defeated by the magic of my ancestors. The source for Allie Mae's unusual strength and range of presence, his vengeance was far deadlier than hers. But I have not thought of the trail of blood Teutates left from Knoxville to Cades Cove in quite some time, as this entity is again bound to the earth where his bones are buried.

I sleep better than I once did, and give thanks for no longer feeling his anger or that of Allie Mae's spirit. Neither one should ever again restlessly traverse the hills and meadows surrounding the cursed ruins of a once beautiful ravine.

May the demon remain a prisoner of peace, and may Allie Mae find solace with her ancestors in the bosom of the Great Spirit.

It is Teutates' brothers and sisters that have pulled my attention as of late, forcing me to again consider the earlier incidents. Danger has come to a sacred place where the four entities' bones lie buried in what once was known as the 'forbidden region' of North Carolina's Smoky Mountains. So says the spirit who once spoke frequently to my grandfather, when he was known to the Cherokee nation as "Two Eagles Cry", a powerful shaman who served his people for almost sixty years. I had only seen the entity once as a child, and never again until shortly after my grandfather's spirit appeared to me in the unholy bowels of Teutates' temple—a lair that had long sat dormant beneath the heart of Cades Cove. When I emerged to salvation from certain death six years ago, the entity stood next to my grandfather's favored avatar as a wolf.

She was just as I remembered her as a young boy.

"Galiena will one day be your guide, and not mine," Two Eagles Cry had told me long ago. And as the wolf played around her feet after Teutates had been vanquished, I realized the day my grandfather spoke of had finally come—many, many years after I had forgotten his prophecy. Evelyn, my granddaughter, has since told me Galiena's uncommon name still exists in rural Italy, though it is rarely given. The pronunciation is the same as it was in ancient Gaul and later in Germania, from where her father, Searix, came, having crossed the Atlantic on a Viking ship…. But I am getting ahead of myself.

"Gal-yan-na" is how to say this name, and it is important to remember. The initial story I am about to relate is largely hers, after I was awakened early this morning with the inspiration to set it down on paper. She has told me it will form the basis to begin a new tale of my own—a journey I will soon share with her. For the past few months, Galiena has increased her visitations—most often in my dreams. Her warnings and pleas have become increasingly more urgent, and I can no longer resist her call to action.

But like every meaningful narrative, one must start at the beginning to fully appreciate the whole. So, we will start with her genesis. The gravity of what I am compelled to deal with in the present has its basis in Galiena's physical life and death. Although it isn't possible to know the exact year of her birth, my best guess is that it took place around the same time the first Crusades ravaged the Holy Land halfway across the world. As touched on earlier, her father journeyed from Germania to the New World. It was a desperate attempt to find lasting freedom for his clan—one with roots that predated Caesar's plunder of his people's homeland. Accompanied by brave and resourceful cousins from Scandinavia, a group of roughly forty men set out to find a place far enough from Europe that a centuries-old curse could finally end.

In order to explain in detail the impact of what her father endured in his mission, Galiena has accessed his memories from the *Akasha* and then transferred them to my mind. Without this assistance, she advised I wouldn't fully appreciate the near-insurmountable trials he and his crew endured to reach America. All done in the name of honor and duty, with the likely possibility none of them would ever see their cherished homeland again.

Searix's family descended from a powerful druid line originally based in Britania, and migrated south to what is now northern France and central Germany in the early days of the Roman occupation of the land of Gaul. This clan was not only given special privileges within the druid hierarchy of priests and priestesses (druidesses), but was also responsible for protecting five ossuaries since before the time of Jesus Christ.

Inside these five portable 'tombs' laid the bones of five unusual humanoids—considered by many as deities due to their abilities to manifest in physical form from time to time after these mysterious creatures were no longer alive. Galiena gave me the names of these entities—two females known as Abnoba and Brigindo, and three males named Abelio, Smetrios, and Teutates—the ringleader of them all. According to Galiena, Abnoba and Abellio were forest entities needed to balance the warlord god, Smetrios, and equally violent goddess, Brigindo. Of course, Teutates was by far the most powerful and wicked among them all.

For reasons unexplained by my precocious spirit guide, after almost a thousand years of complex rituals successfully keeping the gods and goddesses in check when they would periodically awaken from their slumber, suddenly these entities began physically manifesting themselves more frequently. The events were followed by wanton bloodshed during the night when clan members were asleep. Mornings would bring bitter anguish to find loved ones torn apart and drained of their blood.

By the time Searix was born, his extended family that had grown to include Vikings from the north, Franks to the west, and other Germanians and Italians to the east and south had been dealing with nocturnal attacks from their protected deities for more than two hundred years. Attempts to dispose of the bloody pestilence failed miserably. Every effort to remove the bones from the clan's presence had resulted in increasingly violent reprisals from the five ill-tempered spirits. And, attempts to take the ossuaries hundreds of miles away brought swift retaliation much worse than the punishment administered for shorter distances from the villages.

Finally, after an especially violent series of attacks had claimed the lives of nearly one hundred people, a plan was devised to take the demons far away from civilization. To a fabled place located beyond the western horizon, where seafaring men were said to survive only after being "lifted by angels" to the shores of this mysterious new land.

Fearless in his youth and status as the oldest son of the clan's most revered patriarch, Searix volunteered for the mission to take the five ossuaries as far west as possible. His confidence in burying the entities' vile remains in this fabled new world was very strong. His Viking cousins were the first to join him, and he quickly gathered the rest of his crew from among the warriors who served his father. All were eager to find this mysterious place so often talked about, though none had ever seen the smallest evidence of its existence.

Galiena couldn't tell me the specifics of dates and times, and the calendars used by this clan were somewhat unique compared to what we have now. But from what I could decipher from environmental clues, the crew set sail in early spring, and despite many temptations to return home, Searix and his men reached the shores of what would eventually become North Carolina by mid-summer. Roughly three months at sea, the crew was near starvation when they stood upon dry land for the first time since leaving Europe. It took more than a week to regain enough sustenance to resume the task of finding a new 'home' for the five hated entities. Along the way to the New World, they had lost two men to mysterious illnesses, and those aboard the ship believed Teutates and his siblings had a hand in the men's deaths.

Thirty men headed into the forest, and the hope was to return within the next two months. But it took much longer.

A sensitive named Adalbern was counted on to let them know when they had reached the right spot to bury the five ossuaries. Searix had inherited strong intuitive gifts as well. Yet to everyone's surprise, they didn't reach a suitable spot traveling through the mountainous terrain until November. By then, the group had encountered North America's indigenous peoples—a race of red-skinned humans who regarded them with as much curiosity as the white-skinned Europeans had for these early natives from the north. Both were exploring the uncharted mountains while keeping a respectful distance from one another.

I recognized the landmarks of the ravine that would later become the ill-fated lovers' lane of Cades Cove. It was there that the weary travelers from Germania and Scandinavia decided they had found the right place. Perhaps the entire quintet of ornery deities would have found a final resting place there, though I shudder to think of what Allie Mae's wraith would have been like had she possessed more than Teutates' power when she went on her rampage. While preparing the chosen spot to lay the main demon's ossuary, one of the men carrying it lost his footing and the portable tomb for Teutates shattered upon contact with the unforgiving rocky earth.

Watching through Searix's eyes the ink-like essence drift high into the air after escaping its prison was an especially uncomfortable experience for me, recalling my own dealings with Teutates. It mattered little that this was the memory of another man in another time…. Searix's small army scurried about in panic while hastily gathering Teutates' grotesquely misshapen skeleton. They buried it in the very spot later excavated by the team of University of Tennessee scientists attempting to recover what was left of Allie Mae McCormick's crushed remains—bones that fate had placed atop a monster's.

Afterward, the men gathered the remaining four ossuaries and fled the ravine—but not before several of their comrades were pulled back by the thickening mist that pursued the group out of the ravine with a vengeance. The victims' shrieks of agony filled the air as they succumbed to Teutates' murderous wrath. I watched through Searix's eyes as the rest of the men didn't stop running for many miles, and waited to set camp until the next morning. Sleeping until mid-afternoon, the surviving twenty-six men worked through the night, and not wanting to risk another attack from Teutates, they repeated this process until the group stumbled upon another ravine—this one carrying a stronger tranquil sense than the one in Cades Cove.

Searix and Adalbern took this as a positive omen from the noble gods they worshipped, and they waited anxiously for the morning's sunlight to return. Then they dug through the snow with their swords, spades, and tree limbs, working diligently to place the remains of Abnoba, Bridingo, Abellio, and Smetrios in each of the four corners of the ravine's basin. This time the ossuaries remained intact.... But no sooner than the men headed into the forest's depths toward the Atlantic coast, the four formerly peaceful gods and goddesses from the Gallic pantheon emerged from their new home. Although lacking the full physical presence that Searix had witnessed in the attacks on his village, he recognized the essences of Brigindo and Smetrios—the deities most prone to physical violence. Their rage matched that of Teutates two weeks earlier. Searix's warnings fell on deaf ears, and when the mist-like fingers of Brigindo decapitated Adalbern, the rest of the men ran in terrible fear.

The carnage was extensive, leaving just a dozen survivors. The last of the men stayed close together, traveling as much as possible each day and night during their return journey to the Atlantic coast. Covering ten to twenty miles each day, Searix and twelve survivors finally approached the North Carolina shore. To their amazement, their boats were still docked in the sand, although covered in mid-December's snow. And to their immense joy, the mother ship remained anchored a few hundred feet out from shore. If they could reach the boats and navigate the choppiness and bitter cold breeze from the ocean, they had a possibility of making it home safe—a chance that none of them expected.

But the mad dash to reach the boats was interrupted by the blur of the four entities' essences pursuing the men from behind once more. Those who made it to the boats had a head start over those who were cut down along the beach. However, before any of the boats made headway into the ocean, the stealth-like mists were already moving through the water, hovering as an angry boil below the surface. When the bubbling water reached the boats, they were overturned and the men pulled down shrieking into the frigid ocean.

Only one man survived to watch the mother ship speed away. Surely the wary crew inside the ship realized their only shot at survival was to flee, as their comrades along the shoreline were either dead or dying. They left Searix to watch the departure, shivering in the cold from behind a small clump of barren trees near the forest's edge. Brigindo had knocked him down earlier, not long after she fully materialized. But rather than seek to end his life and convert him into a bloody meal, she had moved on to another man, whose larger frame apparently offered more nourishment. Ashamed he didn't try to come to another's rescue and die valiantly, Searix watched as the rest of his crew were finished off by the bloodthirsty quartet.

Before their essences dissipated, Brigindo—who appeared as an exceptionally tall, statuesque woman with alabaster white skin, braided blonde hair, and pupil-less lavender eyes turned to look in Searix's direction. She smiled, and I could feel his horror in seeing twin rows of sharp, pointed teeth glistening with blood. He cowered instinctively, cursing his faltering courage beneath his breath.

Searix sought to better camouflage his presence from her and the others, though obviously too late. He didn't dare look again as she approached, but heard a light chuckle… then silence. When the maddening wait for a forthcoming punishment never materialized, he tentatively opened his eyes. The four entities had just reentered the forest from which they came. Searix didn't venture from his inadequate hideout until the winter sun reached its highest point.

Iroquois Indians captured him the next day, and brought the lone survivor of the Europeans to their main village in the Smokies. Although difficult at first, Searix eventually was able to communicate with the tribe's hierarchy. A shaman of considerable talent, named "Twin Bears" took a liking to Searix, and the two became friends and eventually family.

Allowed to keep his Germanian name and customs, Searix ultimately courted and married Twin Bears' daughter. Unfortunately, their only child, Galiena, would never make it to full adulthood. Killed during a raid from an enemy tribe, she was mistaken as a male due to her fondness for war paint and the weapons carried by the tribe's warriors. Her grieving parents and the rest of the tribe moved farther west to be less vulnerable to attacks.

But Galiena's spirit remained behind, drawn by a sense of obligation to protect her people. She sensed the four restless deities lurking in the ravine, located a few miles from the Iroquois village now abandoned and still close enough to be a menace to where the tribe relocated. She made a pact with the Great Spirit to protect the innocent from these vile entities forevermore.

I have heard that time passes quickly on the other side of the veil… I certainly hope so. Otherwise, Galiena's successful thousand-year reign as guardian of this ravine might seem unfair—especially now that a millionaire land developer named Simon Blankenship has unwittingly reawakened the four demon-deities after a millennium of peace.

It's the reason I must journey to Cherokee, North Carolina in hopes of stopping the drilling to lay sewage pipes in this sacred ravine. Galiena has warned me that I can no longer delay the visit to the place known to my ancestors as *Tsvsgina Odalv*, or Devil Mountain. "The opportunity to stop the madman from unleashing Hell on Earth is slipping!" she urges. "Come, Running Deer—come *now!*"

So, I must leave this morning... the very day David and Miriam Hobbs have come to spend time in Cades Cove. They have returned for the first time in six years, with two of their kids, looking forward to spending time with Evelyn and me during the Fourth of July holiday and a week beyond.... But they will be in grave danger if the entities are released and come here in search of Teutates, their lord. We will *all* be in terrible straights if that event comes to pass.

I have convinced Evelyn to stay and entertain the Hobbs in my absence for a few days, while I try to save an idiot from not only hurting himself and his employees, but also hurting my people living near the land they rejected from their allotment when the reservation was created. No one was to ever own it, and it sat abandoned until the Supreme Court ordered the United States Park Service to return it to the Malcolm Blankenship estate two years ago, to which Simon Blankenship is the only living heir.

No man was to ever lay claim upon this land. And, now, what was once allowed to sleep for centuries in peace is wide-awake... and hungry.

May God help us all.

John Running Deer

Chapter One

Evelyn was greatly displeased with me for going to North Carolina.

We shared what some would call an 'animated discussion' after breakfast that lasted the better part of an hour. What prompted her ire was my stated intention to travel to Cherokee later that morning. My original plan was to stay a few days to try to convince Simon Blankenship to alter his sewer line's path so that it circumvented the ravine in question instead of cutting directly through it.

"Grandpa," she said. "Have you not been listening to what I've been telling you for the past week?"

"Yes, I have listened closely to everything you have mentioned—even the card reading I didn't voluntarily participate in," I replied, offering what I thought was a playful look.

"Then you understand the severity of what you'll face if they are waiting for you—and they are."

Evelyn's stare is formidable, since her lovely deep brown eyes can bore deeply into a man's soul. I felt the pin pricks along my spine and upon the crown of my head as she sought access to my mind. Not easy for an old man like me to hide from… although I have managed over the years to keep her prying gaze out of most of my thoughts, surrendering only the mundane whenever possible.

She has scolded me often for shirking my responsibility to my Cherokee kinsman as a shaman—an unwilling one at that. But in truth, *she* is the one with the greatest gifts of seeing beyond the death veil and discerning the future with remarkable clarity. Not to mention her guides are many, and keep her well informed.

So maybe she should be the one visiting the cursed ravine at the foot of Devil Mountain instead of me. Correct?

Perhaps… but she will never venture into the domain of evil, unless presented with no other alternative. She has not forgotten her previous confrontations with Teutates, and her admonishment to me just two days ago was facing these other four deities is like "Teutates times two". Separate from one another, the entities are only slightly stronger than Allie Mae was in her natural anger. But together—especially when led by either Smetrios or Brigindo—the foursome would be far more formidable than Tuetates in his most violent tirades.

I assured her that I would be careful and was unafraid of what I would soon find. The truth lies in the first part of that assurance—not in the latter. I wouldn't be human if I wasn't terrified about a possible face-to-face confrontation with any of the four *anisginas*, or demons.

"Indeed, I do understand the severity, Ms. 'Two Doves Rising'," I teased, hoping by using her Cherokee birth name it would lower the determination to dissuade me. "But Galiena is increasingly urgent with her pleas to come. And my heart of hearts tells me to wait any longer would make things worse for everyone… including *us*."

Evelyn nodded sullenly, her arms folded across her chest. Certainly, her frown was mostly inspired by my decision to forego her warnings—both from earlier in the week and that morning. But my mysterious guide whom my eldest granddaughter could not see, hear, or even sense also spurred on the uneasiness. At times, I could tell Evelyn was skeptical about Galiena's existence, and if not for the spirit's revelations to me about personal secrets my granddaughter had cleverly kept hidden from my own intuitions, along with obscure historical facts from eastern Tennessee and western North Carolina's jaded past, I do believe Evelyn would no more believe in Galiena's authenticity as a spirit guide to my grandfather, and now me, than she would the Man in the Moon. The daughter of Searix would be nothing more than an imaginary playmate for her dear old grandpa.

"You would do best by not getting involved, Grandpa," she said finally. "Do you not remember how you and I both had regrets about being dragged into the mess in Cades Cove? And it was worse—*much* worse the second time. We almost lost Hanna!"

"But we saved David and his family," I countered.

"That's not what I meant, and you know it," she said, drawing a deep breath while shaking her head. "I love them all… I shouldn't have said that."

"It's okay, Evy," I said softly, using the pet name she once loved as a child, but not so much as she grew to adulthood. A sheepish smile was spreading across her face. "But avoiding this any longer could bring something far worse, and the blood of the innocent would be on my head for not trying to prevent it—just as it would've been if you and I had not saved David Hobbs from Allie Mae McCormick's ghost."

That nailed it. Or, it bought me enough space to leave our conversation and load up the Jeep I had purchased the past spring. The journey across the state line to the east would be the vehicle's longest trek so far, which was a good thing, I reasoned. Once my duffel and laptop were loaded in the back, I stepped over to where Evelyn stood in the driveway, observing me from below the large picture window that Allie Mae's vengeful wraith had long ago peered through at David and me huddling by a fire to avoid her pervasive chill.

"I love you," I told her, pleased that she allowed me to give her a hug.

"I love you, too… very much. But I still wish you weren't going." She fought back tears that tore at my heart's resolve, though my mind was already made up. "Or, at least I wish you were taking me with you… you shouldn't do this alone. Besides, you should be enjoying your retirement from the U.S. Park Service in peace."

"I'll be fine—I promise," I assured her, wondering if she failed to account for the paunch I once carried around my middle had mostly melted away since I officially retired five years ago. I am more physically fit now than before my retirement…. Yes, there now is more gray than black in the traditional braids I've worn since a teenager. But looking back at me in the mirror each morning is a spry seventy-three-year-old with the same ornery twinkle in his brown eyes. "I won't do anything foolish—just have a look around and speak to Mr. Blankenship. Galiena won't—"

"Stop, Grandpa—*please.*"

She pulled away from me and headed back to the front door where our beloved husky, Shawn, poked his head through the doorway. Shawn's light blue eyes regarded me as if he thought this was a mistake, too. But at least I knew he could see and hear Galiena, as often his waging tail was what alerted me to the spirit's presence in my cabin when she'd arrive for a visit.

"What do you want me to tell David and Miriam, again?" Evelyn asked, peering at me through her long dark hair while reaching down to stroke Shawn's neck. He pulled away and disappeared inside the cabin.

"Tell them I will be back no later than Friday evening, the third," I said, repeating what I had told her at breakfast. "Maybe sooner, if I can get everything taken care of tomorrow and the next day. Regardless, we'll have a wonderful Fourth of

July celebration, Evelyn—provided I take care of this first." I added what I hoped was a confidant smile. To my relief, she returned the smile and reminded me to call her when I arrived in Cherokee.

Other than the scenic drive through the mountains, it turned out to be the easy part of my day.

Not long after I made it to the back roads that would take me to Highway 441, Galiena appeared next to me in the passenger seat. The air often brings a slight charge when she is about to manifest her presence. In the process of trying to hang on to the crackling signal from a country music station in Knoxville when I felt a sudden coolness touch my right wrist.

"You know… if you could find a way for Evelyn to at least sense your presence, my life would be a helluva lot easier."

I gave my futile radio station rescue a rest and leaned back in my seat. Galiena hadn't fully materialized yet, but I could tell she was grinning.

"In time, Running Deer," she replied, her musical voice carrying the soft tinny quality that spirits often have. Sometimes her vocal clarity is pristine, but most often she sounds like this. "She's not ready to receive me. Evelyn fears why I am here, and has for quite some time."

Well, that was a newsflash. I wondered why my granddaughter withheld this information from me, as I had assumed some other reason was behind Evelyn's inability to communicate with the favored guide of my grandfather.

"She is curious enough to have researched everything you've told me about concerning your father, Searix, and your Iroquois roots," I said, something I had discussed with the spirit before. "She can't possibly fear you as much as you think."

"Who is the guide here, and who is the stubborn man?" she chided me.

"Touché," I chuckled until I noticed her frown. "What?"

"She is right… there is danger," Galiena advised. "And, there will be times that I can't be with you like this. Still, I will keep an eye on you and guide your mind. Listen to your thoughts—especially when you hear my voice inside your head. Hear me and discern, Running Deer…. They are all awake, and one has escaped. Brigindo is no longer in her prison, and I don't know why…."

Her voice trailed off, sounding forlorn. Admittedly, her discomfort heightened my own misgivings, although I knew the moment I set out on this trip there would be no going back empty handed. I prayed it didn't mean an angry Gallic deity would be chasing me home.

I should mention here that most often Galiena appears in the form and attire of her earthly self at the time of her physical death. As I touched on at the very beginning of this account, she died dressed and marked as a warrior—like the male cousins she admired on her mother's side. Her naturally light skin came from her father, along with piercing blue eyes. She would be quite attractive by modern standards, despite the shaved sides of her head to mimic the young warriors of her tribe. Her light brown hair also came by way of Searix, while her facial features were an even mix from both parents. The ornamental beading in her hair also reflected both ethnic perspectives.

But the war paint spoke to the heritage from this continent, and surely the dark paste surrounding her eyes made her an easy target for the marauders invading her village with murderous intent. In hindsight, perhaps it would've been worse had she been perceived as a beautiful light-skinned girl lurking behind the warrior disguise….

"They won't see me as you do," she said, interrupting my musing of how I would later describe her appearance in my journal. "Without the heart to heart, the picture is different." She pointed at my chest after touching hers. Symbolism that works for all cultures.

I can imagine my audience wondering if we speak in the tongues of our forefathers. The answer is no, since the dialects that would eventually evolve into my ancestors' language went through many changes from Galiena's time. In fact, even the modern Iroquois would struggle to understand words and meanings from her tribe that had been away from their northern brethren for a few hundred years as they migrated south. Yes, we have tried to speak in our native tongues anyway—or at least I have done so, after I encountered her waiting for me to awaken in my hospital bed after the battle with Teutates. She replied to my Cherokee question in English, and mostly to the question foremost in my mind rather than the one I voiced.

"You might be surprised," I told her. "Not everyone out there is closed-minded, and if I do justice to your description...." I didn't finish, since I knew she was right. The only way to fully appreciate Galiena is to know her, and that's an 'invitation only' privilege granted to an exclusive few.

She laughed softly, but said nothing more about it. We chatted briefly about the scenic terrain, and how it had changed over the centuries. Since I wanted to visit the ravine first, I drove past Cherokee and headed north, and when I closed to within a few miles of my destination, Galiena's essence began to evaporate from the Jeep.

Perhaps she also sensed the powerful foreboding that embraced my entire being as I drove along a ridge beyond the northern edge of the reservation—one that offered a spectacular view of *Tsvsgina Odalv.*

"Devil Mountain... there it is," I whispered reverently, turning to the empty seat next to me.

I pointed to the bluish mountain nestled in the midst of smaller hills as if my spirit companion was still beside me. But her seat remained vacant. The intangible aspects of her essence that normally hung in the air were gone. Meanwhile, the feeling of dread grew worse as I exited the highway and veered onto a service road that appeared to be a recent addition to the area. I followed it until I came to the "Blakenship Pines" brick sign that marked the entrance to the subdivision.

"Here goes nothing," I whispered under my breath and entered the gates left standing wide open.

There weren't any signs of anyone working that Wednesday afternoon, but it looked like the new development would soon have a bevy of tenants. Luxurious cabins graced both sides of the winding drive, spaced apart from one another by several acres of tall pines and other trees spared during construction. I had expected the proposed new neighborhood in the middle of the wilderness to be no further than halfway along. Seeing the actual progress was alarming, especially since several of the spectacular homes looked ready for immediate occupancy.

Evelyn had told me they were all million-dollar homes, and seeing the outside workmanship's excellence gave promise that the inside of these log mansions could be even grander than their façades. If not for the prevailing uneasiness gripping the very core of my soul, I might've lingered longer along the road to try and take it all in—this modern 'beautification' of land believed to be cursed by my ancestors for as long as they've resided in these mountains. But I needed to find the ravine, praying it would be obvious and not one of many in this secluded area.

I had an image of what the ravine should look like that came to me via a dream the week before, and confirmed twice by Galiena herself. Given the symbolism in most dreams, I didn't expect the place I sought to jump out at me. Yet it did, once I ignored the immense homes overlooking the ravine from either side.

Perhaps it would've been obvious to find had I merely closed my eyes… the *un*-holiness of the place was palpable, repelling me from looking at it for long. Industrial graders, shovels, and loaders were parked along the edge, and the earth that had been undisturbed since the end of the tenth century lay torn open. It already seemed impossible to protect the four buried ossuaries from sustaining damage.

I parked next to the ravine, carefully scanning the area as I got out of the Jeep. I felt dirty… like I was guilty of trespassing and completely unwanted—an intruder in every sense. My legs felt weak, fed by a swarm of mental pictures alternating between the dangerous entities' home just a few feet away and the knowledge I could soon be escorted from the premises by armed guards… or worse. I made it close enough to see the extent of the work already done. The rips in the earth had torn out a number of trees and pushed aside boulders I recognized from what Galiena had shown to me in her visions. Apparently, the work had started Monday, and I felt a different kind of guilt—that of true regret for waiting so long to get involved.

"Hey, buddy… what in the hell do you think you're doing here?" asked a gruff voice from behind me. I slowly turned around to find a pair of security guards pointing guns in my direction, one a pistol and the other a double-barrel shotgun.

"I'm looking for Simon Blankenship," I announced, offering a warm smile to sell the half-truth and hoping it distracted the two men from detecting my nervousness and quickened heart rate.

I sensed indifference emanating from the youngest one, a short blonde man with curly hair and scruffy beard. His eyes were shaded by dark sunglasses, as were the eyes of the older guard, who stood much taller and carried a pronounced gut—aspects along with his graying close-cropped hair that were non-threatening. But the bigger man's heart carried hatred, and likely directed at my Native American heritage. No, this is not racial oversensitivity... I saw the joy in his mind in response to an imagined physical confrontation with me, to where he filled my chest with the contents of both barrels from his shotgun.

"Well, he ain't here, asshole," said the taller one, whose voice had announced my trespass moments before. "You've got thirty seconds to get out of here. You got that?"

"Yes." I tentatively stepped toward the Jeep. "Perhaps he is still at the office. I'll check for him there."

"You do that," he said, motioning menacingly with his gun to where I feared the damned thing might accidentally discharge... or maybe would *look* like it didn't go off in my direction intentionally. "You damned Indians need to give it a rest and stay the hell away from here.... You got that?"

I nodded and climbed into the Jeep, trying to ignore new mental pictures emanating toward me from the shotgun wielding guard of him blowing a hole through the rear of the Jeep that also removed my head. I waved politely as I left, believing this jerk wouldn't dare shoot me while driving away.... But then he aimed his gun and motioned to his little buddy to do the same. Thankfully, I was far enough away by the time junior caught his elder's drift, to where accuracy would be an issue. Neither one launched a shot.

"Whew! That was stupid, John!" I scolded myself, offering thanks that neither one carried a high-powered rifle instead of the pedestrian weapons they were armed with.

My heart continued to pound until I was back on the highway and headed to Cherokee. I had the address for Blankenship Enterprises programmed into the Jeep's GPS, and would arrive within the next twenty minutes or so. The dashboard's clock read 12:42 p.m., and I anticipated Mr. Blankenship might be at lunch if I were to arrive before two o'clock. I worried about missing him altogether if he were the type of guy who preferred late lunches that meant taking the rest of the afternoon off for recreational fun, like golf or bedding a secretary or two. Evelyn had brought me up to speed Sunday night on Blankenship's long string of indiscretions that had earned him several divorces and many more enemies, both personally and in business.

A prominent local millionaire, he didn't need the money or prestige that could come from building the cabin estates in the subdivision named after him. I worried his ambitions were inspired by his ancestor, Malcolm Blankenship, whose reported deep-seated disdain for the Federal government had been especially acerbated following the Civil War. 'Reconstruction' had been unkind to the Blankenship family throughout the south, and many had been ruined financially. It came as no surprise, then, that the ruthlessly unethical Simon Blankenship decided to turn the screws on the United States government, after discovering land deeds belonging to Malcolm were never considered when the Great Smoky Mountain National Park was chartered in 1934.

Blankenship's lawyers fought hard to get a district court ruling overturned in his favor, and then the Supreme Court decided favorably for Blankenship as well…. But the fact this was not some misguided attempt to add something special to the region, and instead was Simon thumbing his nose while finding a new way to pad his fortune, told me that I wasn't going to find a sympathetic audience for my request to reroute the pipes in the ravine. Blankenship wouldn't care about potential dangers based on 'superstitions' and Native American legends. An ethical appeal wouldn't work either, and I would have to be quite clever in my approach with this man.

Unfortunately for me, meeting with Simon Blankenship would have to wait.

"I'm sorry, he didn't come into the office today," his office manager, Julie Persinger, announced. "Can I help you with something?"

"No, ma'am… my business is with Simon only," I told her, feeling a knot form in the pit of my stomach. "Will he be in tomorrow?"

"I'm not sure," she said. "And you are?"

"My name is John Running Deer. I have something to share with him to make his life easier with the local Indians," I said, determined to sound as non-Native American as possible, despite the fact I clearly am one and the same.

"You could tell me and I can pass it on for you," she offered. The instinctive warning for secrecy that had come over me the moment Ms. Persinger first spoke grew tenfold.

"No, ma'am. What I have to share is solely intended for Mr. Blankenship, since he alone will know how to implement the advice."

It was a calculated risk, since her dislike of me skyrocketed behind her frozen smile. But had I given the message to her, it would've ended up in a wastebasket that afternoon. Dismissing her personal usefulness might trigger enough anger to get the guy I sought an audience with to take time from his nefarious activities and meet the "Indian asshole" who pissed off his office manager. For the sake of my people, and the innocent of all races, I remain willing to fully denigrate myself. If it can prevent an ominous disaster, then it's well worth it.

"Tell you what, Mr. Running Deer…. If Simon comes in tomorrow morning, I'll see what I can do about getting you a meeting," she said, her tone much cooler than her initial greeting. "Do you have a business card?"

"I do, but it's in my car," I said, hoping she wouldn't persist in having me retrieve it for her, since it didn't exist. This was a pissing contest I couldn't afford to lose. "Either of you can reach me at this number."

After I wrote it down, I didn't wait to see what she did with it, politely taking my leave of her presence. Fortunately, my 'second sight' works well in this latter stage of life. I watched Ms. Persinger through my mind's eye as I climbed back into the Jeep. She debated for almost five minutes if she should tear up the piece of paper I wrote my number on, or hang onto it....

With an annoyed chuckle, she finally wrote something next to my phone number and placed the piece of paper in Mr. Blankenship's office mailbox. The only variable now was *when* he would call... hopefully in time to make a difference.

Chapter Two

Simon Blankenship called me that night. Trouble was, he decided to do it after midnight, and he used what Evelyn told me Thursday morning was a standard 'backdoor' cell number to leave a message. I never heard the phone ring since he bypassed that function.

"You mean the bastard wasn't just calling late in hopes I wouldn't pick up the phone and talk to him?"

I was seething from the brush-off handled by a yellow cur—which in hindsight I should've expected, given the man's ethical standards.

"Sorry, Grandpa... I guess the trip out there wasn't the best idea," said Evelyn, on the other end of the line. Her tone was compassionate and lacked any gloating 'I told you so' that could've been there instead. "It sounds like Blankenship has no intention of speaking with you, and definitely won't be willing to meet you in person."

She was right—at least based on the face value of the voicemail.... *"This message is for Mr. John Running Deer.... Julie told me you stopped by today, and sir, I just have to be honest with you. I haven't got time to discuss anything with you, or any other Indians. Sorry to say I heard about your presence at Blankenship Pines this afternoon, and we have already been through this nonsense about building on sacred grounds—despite no Native American mounds or any other Indian sites being located on the property. From here on out, if you have any other concerns, please contact our attorney, David Lavine in Charlotte at 704-528...."*

"Simon Blankenship is a fool!" I said, more harshly in tone than I intended, drawing a glance from several patrons looking up from their breakfast plates. "Sorry. I'm just irritated."

"It's okay, Grandpa," Evelyn assured me. "You told me last night that if you could meet with him today, then you would be on your way back to Tennessee by tonight. Now that you won't be meeting with him any time soon, you'll be coming back home sometime today. Right?"

I couldn't immediately confirm that answer. At the moment, I was sitting in a café across the parking lot from the Best Western I stayed at the night before. Having only a light appetite after a restless night, I reflected on the strange dreams that followed an afternoon and evening of uneasiness.

The accommodations were very good, and in a more peaceful time I might be agreeable to staying at this hotel in the future. But after leaving Blankenship's office, the feeling of being watched and studied from an angry point of view awaited my return to the Jeep. There was no mistaking the hostility of a spirit that had latched on to my ride from the last place I visited: The ravine at Blankenship Pines.

The feeling intensified—like a pair of invisible glaring eyes from somewhere in the rear of the vehicle. Whatever it was, I couldn't detect anything beyond the discomfort. No voices or mental images, and no apparitions materializing or moving items inside the Jeep. The gooseflesh rose painfully, along with a lasting chill along the back of my neck causing the small hairs to flex repeatedly as they stood on end.

I had hoped Galiena would reappear, or at least rejoin me with the warmth of her essence. But whatever had caused her to retreat earlier still held sway. Even my soft vocal entreaties to her—which often coaxed her out of hiding—went ignored.

After I arrived at the hotel and checked in, I enjoyed a short reprieve from the hostile presence. Yet, as soon as I returned to my room after dinner, the hostility was waiting for me, like a silent assassin lurking in the shadows. The room was cold, too, despite the air conditioner being turned off. Watching TV and skimming through a courtesy newspaper did little to distract from floor creaks and furniture pops resounding every few minutes. Meaningful sleep proved to be impossible, despite employing basic cleansing rituals I learned long ago as a boy from my grandfather….

"Grandpa… are you still there?"

"Yes, Evelyn, I'm here."

"So, what are you planning to do next?"

"Well… I am going to try connecting with Mr. Blankenship one last time before leaving."

"And if he blows you off again, will you please give it up for now?"

Evelyn's effort to hide her irritation beneath a thick layer of compassion was admirable.

"Yes… I'll give it up for now and come home."

My commitment carried the truest intentions, and Evelyn moved on to tell me the Hobbs clan arrived at the cabin well after midnight—likely not long after Simon Blankenship sought to covertly dispose of my request to speak with him in person. My granddaughter gave up the room she once shared with Hanna for Jillian Hobbs to sleep in, and Chris was more than content with the rollaway upstairs in the loft. David and Miriam took my bed, leaving Evelyn the pullout sofa in the living room.

Not the most optimal arrangements, but it was only for the first two nights. The Hobbs' reservation for a spacious chalet in the hills overlooking Gatlinburg didn't start until Friday. The Fourth of July had become a very popular event in the region, and in some ways rivaled the onslaught of visitors in October and at Christmas.

"Tell David, Miriam, and the kids I look forward to seeing them tonight." I tried to sound excited, pushing aside the nagging fear I should've attempted to reschedule the Hobbs' vacation once Galiena stepped up her warnings about the impending trouble in North Carolina nearly a month ago. I regretfully misjudged the seriousness and potential consequences.

"I will, Grandpa." Evelyn sounded relieved.

With my granddaughter's peace of mind taken care of, I set out to make the most of the remaining few hours in Cherokee. Getting a face-to-face meeting with Simon Blankenship, however, remained unattainable.

The disagreeable persona lurking beneath Julie Persinger's professional façade from Wednesday afternoon morphed into Theodora from *Oz the Great and Powerful* soon after I returned to Blankenship Enterprises. Realizing it was a lost cause to make any headway with her or her equally congenial boss, who was nowhere to be found, I did the only other mischievous thing I could think of.

I revisited the construction site.

Perhaps it wasn't the smartest decision, but I needed one last look at the place. Maybe it was for my own peace of mind. Or, maybe this was Galiena's subtle suggestion from afar. Regardless, once I made the choice to return to the ravine I quit worrying about any threats against my person, whether spiritual or physical.

The main gates were again wide open, and I drove through them casually, prepared to ask for the site supervisor if the guards or other employees stopped my progress. To my surprise, I made it all the way to the ravine without seeing a soul, and I found it ironic that the first new residents I encountered were a trio of young kids playing in their backyard overlooking the ravine. Their new home was the largest cabin I had seen thus far.

I returned the kids' calls to me with a friendly wave after getting out of the Jeep, wondering if they could feel the intense hostility emanating from the ravine's basin. Additional construction equipment had been added since yesterday, crowding the easement. The concerted effort to dig up the rest of the ravine seemed eminent.

Hoping the kids would soon ignore my presence, I turned my attention to where the boulders and tree roots had been recently exposed.

That's when I saw it.

"Holy shit," I murmured in dismay. Though I stood too far away for anything other than a general view, one of the ossuaries appeared to have been broken. I could see shattered pieces from what looked like a stone lid lying in the dirt next to a similar stone box.

Regretfully, I had forgotten to bring along my camera that has a great zoom lens. But then I recalled my cell phone included a camera function Evelyn had recently shown to me. I eagerly dug the phone out of my pants pocket, remembering how she used her index finger and thumb across the phone's screen when in camera mode to create a zoom affect. I did that now and pointed it at the broken ossuary. The left edge of the ruptured ossuary soon appeared on the screen. I snapped several pictures of this while continuing to enlarge the image. I could only shake my head at the dark, mud-covered bones peering out through the box's wound. I snapped two more shots, along with a close-up view of the lid's largest shard. A series of familiar symbols-- either letters or pictograms—were engraved upon it.

The language of Teutates!

Footsteps approached softly from behind. I froze.

28

"You must have a serious death wish, mister."

It wasn't the voice from yesterday. Something told me this fact was fortuitous, as otherwise I might already be dead.

"For taking pictures of an old ravine?" I smiled as I turned to face the owner of the voice... a man in his late fifties, by my guess. Dark haired with pronounced jowls, mirrored sunglasses shaded the man's eyes. He smiled and shook his head when I shrugged and held my hands out to show I meant no harm to anyone.

"Smitty and Roger said they'd just as soon shoot you dead rather than deal with you again," said the man, motioning for me to step away from the ravine. "You were here yesterday, and they'll be back in about ten minutes. So, you best be gettin' on out of here."

"I suppose I should thank you, huh?"

"For what?"

"For saving my life." I chuckled and he joined me. "John Running Deer."

"Amos Johnson," he said, reluctantly shaking my hand. His grip was like holding a freshly dead fish. No backbone to either one. "What brings you here, Mr. Running Deer?"

"Apparently, I'm too late," I said, deciding on giving the truth... at least in a small dose. "It would be better to circumvent the ravine to complete the sewer line, to avoid the boulders and other debris buried here for centuries. Blankenship Pines would be finished sooner."

Amos Johnson eyed me curiously, and I sensed his surprise in not only my knowing what the hold-up was about, but also suggesting the best solution to get things back on track. At least that's what I gathered from the images I picked up from his thoughts.

"You really should go now," he said, his voice lacking any of the malevolence I encountered from his peers the previous afternoon. "I don't want to see anyone get hurt."

I moved to the Jeep and climbed inside, watching this man slowly trudge toward a construction trailer I hadn't noticed. Our entire encounter lasted only a few minutes, and during that time I felt the heat of invisible anger emanating toward us from the desecrated tomb intensify. I could've mentioned it... but what good would it do? If these employees of Simon Blankenship cared about such a crime, or even the archaeological significance of the ossuary itself, there wouldn't have been a fractured tomb with bones sticking out of it for me to witness.... And as for reporting something like this to the local authorities? I couldn't risk possible jail time for ignoring warnings to stay away.

But the game plan would have to change now that the breach had been verified. We had to move quickly, and yet my heart told me it would be too difficult to get one of the better Native American associations out here in time to halt the damage and heal the desecration. All we could do in the immediate moment was pray for a miracle... that the entity whose bones were disturbed would take pity on the foolish humans responsible.

As I exited Blankenship Pines, I beseeched the Great Spirit to have mercy on those at risk, such as the three youngsters at play in the vicinity of wickedness that had long ago feasted on the blood of other children in the land of Gaul. Even Amos, Smitty, and Roger deserved protection from a force far more formidable than any of them could begin to imagine....

It wasn't until I approached the Tennessee border that I began to relax. The unwelcome voyeur that had shadowed me since yesterday pulled back, as if the spirit wasn't allowed to follow me all the way home. But as I resolved to locate my beloved country music station once again, my fingers were grazed by coolness that cut to the bone.

Galiena had returned.

But before I could rebuke her (playfully) for leaving me high and dry against both human and spiritual menaces, I detected instability in her materialization. Her open mouth was trembling.

Is she crying?

This was something I had never seen before…. Galiena was obviously terribly upset, and trying to say something.

"What is it, my friend?" I asked tenderly, alarmed by her behavior.

She sobbed in silence, but also mouthed something. Something familiar. Something Cherokee.

"Didayolihvdvgalenisgv!"

"Huh?"

"Didayolihvdvgalenisgv . Adatlisvi Awiinageehi!"

Galiena had rarely addressed me in my native tongue, since we both stumbled when trying to navigate each other's dialects. But even considering that struggle, there was no mistaking the message given to me now.

"Goodbye… Goodbye, Running Deer."

She was far too distraught to explain what she meant by her words, leaving me no choice but to wait it out. Wait and pray that I soon learned what prompted her words and tears, all the while more and more certain that coming to North Carolina was a regrettable and irreversible mistake.

Chapter Three

Goodbye was not meant in an immediate sense.

Galiena's message didn't portend her intent to leave me as my guide.... When she calmed down enough to clarify her statement, it wasn't her that would be leaving. It was *me*. The threat came from the entity holding Galiena at bay—Abellio. His sister, Brigindo, had begun reclaiming her freedom from degrees of bondage that had restricted her ability to thrive in the physical world for more than a millennium.

I now knew for certain which entity's presence had been tagging behind me like an ornery puppy with a mean streak. Brigindo's initial frailties in manifestation would soon end, according to Galiena. In a matter of days—if not hours—Brigindo would regain a strong enough foothold in our world to begin feeding herself until she regained the physical form she once enjoyed in ancient times.

Just like Teutates. *Shit!*

"I am sorry Running Deer." Galiena's voice was subdued, barely audible, but at least the tears had ceased to fall. When my spirit friend materialized fully, she appeared as solid as any living, warm-blooded human being.

Near-matching streams stretched from her eyes to her jaw-line. But the moisture from her tears quickly evaporated—a key telltale aspect that separates the living from the dead. Physical changes can morph in the blink of an eye for the deceased, and I have become convinced that spirits walk among us all on a daily basis when fully manifested. But unless we are truly paying attention to such small details, we often can't tell the difference between those individuals who have warm blood pumping through their veins and those who are nothing more than a chilled imitation.

"You have nothing to apologize for," I told her, keeping an eye out for my exit from the main highway. "We will figure out something to help those at risk near Cherokee."

I added a reassuring smile, though at the moment I was at a loss as to what I could offer anyone. The one entity was loose, and my gut told me the rest would soon follow. There was nothing I could personally do to help—not any more.

We'd be home within the next twenty minutes, or at least I would. I expected Galiena to leave again at some point, as rarely will she accompany me inside my cabin when I've got company. She prefers Shawn and myself only, and for at least one more day I had a family of four to accommodate, along with Evelyn.

"You don't understand," Galiena replied. "They are all very angry. They might not hold you accountable for what has happened... but I can't be sure. They resented your presence in the ravine, since they understand that if you could find a way, you'd silence them forever."

True. I would do it, if for no other reason than the trio of innocent children at play nearby. The *Akasha* visions Galiena shared with me from Searix's memories were often brutal. The aftermath from the entities' attacks on the villages in ancient Germania was laid out clearly for me. Transferred images of the ravaged and torn bodies of innocent children—dozens of them—will stay with me forevermore.

"Wouldn't you?" I asked, glancing in her direction while keeping an eye on the road ahead. "Wouldn't you stop them, once and for all, if you could figure out how to do it without harming the innocent?"

She nodded, turning her attention away from me.

"They are laughing at you... at us," she said, peering out through the passenger window. "Their bones are like rock—petrified even before my earthly birth—and cannot be destroyed. All four will soon be free of their stone tombs—either by the men determined to dig up the ravine, or they will find other means to destroy the seals holding them as prisoners. Once they are no longer encumbered by the ossuaries and free to go wherever they please, if they decide to pursue you here...what then?"

I hadn't seriously considered the possibility until mentioned by Galiena. It had been a fleeting fear, without substance, that I briefly thought about and dismissed as fanciful.

"We'll deal with that when, or even if, it happens," I said. "After all, you'll be the first person to know what's happening and then let me know before trouble arrives... right?"

My effort to add a reassuring smile must've failed. She shook her head solemnly.

"If they make it here, what will prevent them from blocking me again—like Abellio did the past two days? And when they sense Teutates' remains are buried not far, in the other ravine in Cades Cove...."

Galiena didn't finish her thought, as unnecessary to do so. I thought about our famed local ravine as disturbing images came to mind. The former "lovers' lane" had been destroyed during our past battle with Teutates. His unholy temple collapsed upon itself, and it took an arrangement with the Blount County Fire Department to supervise the burning of the ruined structure and timber within the ravine. To this day, the charred remnants of everything—including the ashes of trees that had borne signatures from over one hundred years ago—represented all that was left of the once pristine area.

Yet, below the deep piles of debris lay the bones of Teutates and his numerous victims from the previous ten centuries. Evelyn and I worked tirelessly to get every local government authority and office available to bind the University of Tennessee from digging them up again, after the Antiquities Department received word of what had been done to the historic site. Once the smoke ceased rising from the ashes, my partners with the local U.S. Park Service and I built a fence around the entire perimeter of the ravine—a barbed-wire barrier with several large signs warning everyone to keep out. Then I set out to forget about it all….

It seemed like a wise choice at the time. Now, however, I'm not so sure. Especially if the other entities, soon to be set free, learned that their leader's bones were buried beneath the ravine's basin.

Galiena chuckled just before we reached Beaver Falls Trail, the road that leads directly to my place.

"What's so funny?" I asked her.

"The pictures in your head," she replied. "But this time I concur... it would've been better for you and your friend Micky Webster to retrieve the bones of Teutates and take them out onto the ocean to be scattered for eternity."

I nodded in silence, considering her keen intuitions had fully discerned the images dominating my thoughts for the past ten minutes or so... and then I grew serious.

"We should've done it," I said, finally. But the passenger seat was empty when I glanced her way again. True to form, she'd bailed on me just as I reached my driveway. "Guess we'll discuss all of this again soon.".

I was certain she heard me. I felt a nudge inside my solar plexus, followed by a message to my brain.

Soon indeed, Running Deer… very soon.

* * * * *

"Well, hello, stranger!" David Hobbs rose to greet me from my cherished rocker. He held a bottle of Killian's fresh from the fridge, tipping the bottle in salute. "It's so good to see you, John!"

"Likewise, my friend." I readily accepted his embrace, adding a hearty slap upon his shoulder. "I'm glad to be back home, and I've been looking forward to your visit since April, when you confirmed y'all would be coming."

"Yeah, I know… we had every intention of making the trip out here this past spring," said David, smiling awkwardly. "I should've booked everything in January, but you know how tax season is for a self-employed CPA these days…. Besides, there's a lot more to do out here in summer."

"The important thing is that all of you are here—safe and sound, and ready to have some fun," I assured him, pausing to nod to Miriam, his lovely wife, who presently shared the sofa with Evelyn.

I recalled Miriam's personal encounter with Teutates, and smiled at how at peace she seemed to be. I was pleased to see the darkness that had long hung over her aura since her personal encounter with the demon monster had finally lifted. Her blue eyes were bright again, although the premature gray that had streaked her long dark hair shortly after the experience remained. Even so, the gratitude for being alive that exuded powerfully from her was stronger than ever.

David seemed more relieved, too, since the last time we had seen each other, although a subtle glint of pain or worry still remained in his warm hazel eyes. *Still thinking about Allie Mae, perhaps?* He, too, hadn't been spared the premature aging to his hair. Always a blonde and one who disdained men's hair color products, patches of gray had crept into his moustache and nearly conquered his sideburns. And, where he was the svelte one when we first met, he was now working on a noticeable beer gut. Somewhat of a health enthusiast back then, his perspective on living a long life had changed. Fears that become chronic, along with the expectation of further retribution from a family curse, can do that to a person.

"You look great, John—have you been working out?" he asked.

"Retirement has been good… mostly," I said. "But Evelyn takes me bicycle riding in Gatlinburg—"

"Don't let him fool you, David. Grandpa walks quite a bit," Evelyn interrupted. "We rarely go into town, except to pick up supplies." She smiled impishly.

"Well, it looks like you can help me get rid of this." David tapped his belly. "Just as long as we stay on the beaten path this time."

"In the park? You know we won't venture any further than we did two summers ago," I said, wondering if something subconscious had triggered the faint reference to the 'place' we had promised to never mention again in each other's company. *The "lovers' lane" ravine is no more… remember?* "Are you up for a short trek? We could visit Abrams Falls"

"Something like that… Chris and Jill have picked out five or six sights to see in the cove," said David, motioning to the pair sitting at the dining room table. "Everything that got rained out the last time is on the menu… right kids?"

Chris Hobbs nodded shyly. Fifteen years old, he looked as if he had grown several inches in height since Evelyn, Hanna, and I visited Littleton, Colorado this past December. Like his older sister, Jillian, he had always favored his father in appearance—largely on account of the same hazel eyes and blonde hair. But now I had a better picture of what David once looked like as a young high schooler.

Jillian, meanwhile, took me aback. She had missed seeing us in December, spending time with her senior pals from

Littleton High School in Breckenridge instead. Evelyn and I hadn't seen her since she graduated from junior high.... Only a slight limp remained from a joint condition she suffered from since childhood, barely noticeable as she stood to come give me a hug. I had become sort of a godfather to her, and had seen occasional photographs. But they did little justice to the beautiful young woman she had become. At eighteen, her hair and eyes matched her younger brother, Chris, but her facial features now favored Miriam's more than David's, as well as her tall slender figure.

"She's really grown up, hasn't she Grandpa?" said Evelyn, admiringly. "She starts classes at Denver University this fall."

"Yes, she has grown up," I said, opening my arms to give her a hug. "You'll be the belle of the ball, as they used to say." She smiled shyly and traded places with Chris, who had also stood. Though I wasn't sure if he wanted a hug or not, I offered one to him. His choice of a handshake brought laughter from everyone.

"Well, I guess that just leaves you, Miriam. Hug or handshake?" I teased.

She stood up for a hug, telling me that Tyler wished he could have joined them, but football camp at the University of Colorado was set to start next week.

"Following in his dad's footsteps, after all?" I grinned at David, who raised his lager in salute.

"He's actually doing it for Norm as much as me, being he has a great chance of starting this year at halfback," said David.

"You don't say?" I said this warmly, though something told me there was disappointment in store for Tyler and his football aspirations. Better to focus on Chris's football future instead. Something very big and bright was coming his way. "I hope Ty does well.... How about you, Chris? You play football, too, don't you?"

"Yeah… but my practice starts in August." He grinned shyly.

"Chris is following David's footsteps as a quarterback, and this is his first year playing," said Miriam. "Evelyn said he will keep growing in stature and has the build of a young Peyton Manning."

"Well… maybe you'll be even better than all three Mannings."

I didn't want to linger too long in this area for fear either David or Miriam would talk more about Tyler and detect my worry for their oldest boy. I noticed Evelyn was studying me, wearing a knowing smirk. I excused myself to get a Killian's, too.

Before long we were grilling steaks in the backyard while Jill and Chris played with Shawn. I could tell Evelyn was dying to interrogate me about what I had discovered in North Carolina, but she hid it well from our company. After dinner we sat on the back deck facing miles of undisturbed forestland, catching up on everything we had missed in one another's lives since the holidays. Even though David and I had spoken fairly often on the phone since then, as had Miriam and Evelyn, there's nothing like a face-to-face visit to get the true lowdown of what's been going on.

Miriam mentioned they were considering relocating to either San Francisco or Savannah, Georgia once Chris was in college. Of course, having my favorite couple residing roughly four hundred miles away on the Atlantic coast instead of the two-thousand-mile distance to California would be my choice. Both were looking to retire early, and wanted a place near the ocean without the hustle and bustle of South Beach and L.A.

"Both places would be exciting cities to come visit you!" Evelyn enthused, which seemed to relieve them both, as if leaving the Denver area without our approval would present some kind of deterrent. Interestingly, the liquor flowed more readily from that point on—except for the kids, of course—and the merriment took us to dusk.

I shooed everyone back inside the cabin while I cleaned up the grill. My granddaughter finally had the opportunity she was looking for.

"You don't think I can see your worry, Grandpa," she told me, after volunteering to take the grilling plate and utensils inside while I scrubbed down the grill. "It's that bad?"

"Yes," I replied without looking up from my task. "I was too late."

"Too late to stop the digging?"

"Worse… too late to prevent the release of the one named Brigindo."

Evelyn gasped.

"I know," I continued. "I'm deeply concerned about the people who have begun moving into their new homes. Hopefully, without their plumbing ready they won't stay the night just yet. Perhaps they're unpacking by day and staying in a Cherokee hotel at night."

"You know as well as I do these are not goblins and ghouls that merely go bump in the night!" Evelyn hissed angrily, her voice hushed for the Hobbs' benefit. "Are you saying Blankenship's people desecrated Brigindo's resting place?"

"Her ossuary is broken. The lid was smashed and I saw the bones protruding from her tomb."

"And Galiena was no help to you?" There was smugness beneath my granddaughter's worry, nearly spurring me to anger.

"It's not her fault, Evelyn," I said, determined to keep my voice down and hoping she did the same. "The one named Abellio held her captive. They are stronger now than they have ever been in Galiena's existence, whether when she was flesh and bone or as the spirit she is now. She is just as alarmed as you and I are about this."

I believe what terrified Evelyn was that she had no previous inkling of how serious things had become in our neighboring state. Lately, her gifts had been reduced to a general awareness instead of the keen details she normally can determine. It was the same thing that had happened when Teutates gained his foothold into our reality years earlier, even after the demon was bound to the ravine again, beneath the cursed ruins where he could no longer torment her.

"They're going to come here," she whispered, as if suddenly afraid that someone, or something, hostile might hear her. "They will come for him in time... Teutates surely knows this."

"You don't think he still sleeps?"

"No... and probably he has been awake since the first night I couldn't sleep," she said, wearily. "We have to contact someone to make Blankenship stop. I will call the Native History Association in the morning to see if they can put me in contact with the North Carolina group that handles the same type of thing. I should contact my AIM friends out west, too, and speak with the elders at the reservation in Cherokee, since our sisters and brothers are at risk.... Hopefully, we can reach someone working tomorrow, if they all haven't left for the holiday weekend."

"They might not be able to do anything, since these are not Native American remains we're dealing with," I said, careful to not come across as condescending. Evelyn was right in trying to find someone to help us. The situation was already too big for the two of us to try and fix on our own, and with Galiena underestimating the entities' power, my granddaughter's legion of guides might also prove ineffective. "I will meditate on it."

"With our company here? Do you seriously expect to find any time for that?"

"There's no other choice."

Evelyn rejoined our cherished guests as I finished my cleanup. But before returning inside the cabin that has been my home for more than forty years, I hung back a moment on the deck with Shawn. We had left the rear security lights off in favor of tiki torches and the deck's recessed lighting I added last summer. In hindsight, maybe the decision to sit in dimness wasn't such a good thing, since it soon brought confirmation of Evelyn's fears.

Shawn noticed it first. In the thick darkness of the forest something approached, snapping twigs and silencing the crickets and cicadas that had entertained us with their choruses swelling and subsiding like the breaths from some enormous invisible creature. I might have questioned my own hypersensitivity if Shawn hadn't growled protectively.

"It's okay, boy… stay close to Daddy."

I reached down to pat his neck and steer him to the back door. All the while, the heated gaze of something menacing pricked the back of my neck similar to what I had experienced in North Carolina the past two days. Whether or not the presence ventured onto my property was hard to determine, as I didn't look over my shoulder, and didn't steal a peek until we were safely inside and I peered out the small window in the backdoor. When I turned on the security lights that immediately banished the darkness to the remote corners of the backyard, my spirit continued to detect hostility still lurking nearby.

I forced myself to turn away and rejoin our friends gathered in the living room. Carrying on as if I hadn't a care in the world, no one—including Evelyn—seemed to notice my deepening worry. For the rest of the night I couldn't shake the feeling that something unwelcome was scouting the perimeter of my home from outside. Even Shawn resisted the urge to take care of his personal business out back until after the dawn's light appeared on the eastern horizon. His whimpering awakened me from where I slept on the recliner.

By then the presence was gone. But if what happened the night before was a harbinger of things to come, we wouldn't have long to find a solution. I prayed for protection, and for enough time to find the right cure for what was brewing before things got noticeably worse… before things turned deadly.

Chapter Four

I didn't talk to Evelyn about Thursday night's experience… at least not right away. She was already upset by the fact she couldn't reach anyone on the contact list she had mentioned earlier.

Hiding our shared apprehension, Friday was spent visiting Cades Cove, sticking to the usual tourist attractions. By the time we had visited Grotto, Laurel and Abrams Falls, the adults in our group were pretty exhausted. Jill and Chris still had plenty of energy to burn, but as I feared, David's lack of physical exercise during the past couple of years was taking a toll.

"How about we head into Gatlinburg and you guys can check out the arcades and go-cart tracks?" David suggested, massaging his lower back as if tender.

"I thought we were going to do Gatlinburg tomorrow?" Jill sounded disappointed, and I was honestly surprised her hip wasn't killing her by now. But she had kept up with Chris and her chronic limp remained absent. Like him, it appeared she was ready to return to the heart of the park for some more hiking—this time to Rainbow Falls.

"We've got Dollywood tomorrow, Jill, in Pigeon Forge," Miriam advised. "Gatlinburg will be on Sunday… and remember we will be coming back here several times before we go back to Colorado."

"Same deal for Gatlinburg and Pigeon Forge, too," added David. He shuffled slowly from the picnic table we were presently gathered around, near the Old Grist Mill. Heading to the Hobbs' rented Chevy Traverse, he gingerly motioned for the rest of us to follow. Miriam hurried to catch up to him, tenderly assisting him into the back seat after taking the keys from his hand.

"May I drive?" asked Evelyn. "Since I know this area really well, it might be easier."

"Sure." Miriam seemed relieved, as her main concern was obviously alleviating David's discomfort.

I had commandeered the front passenger seat until then, but motioned for Miriam to join Evelyn, and I would sit with David in the back. A moment of nostalgia hit me before climbing in, being so close to where I spent much of my time while employed by the U.S. Park Service. In fact, the visitor center near the old mill was where I had spent the 'golden years' of my forty-five-year career as a ranger—mostly serving as a tour guide. It was where my retirement party was held, not long after Micky and I had 'quarantined' the ravine to the best of our ability.

"Should we hire a masseuse for you tonight?" I teased David.

"Okay... the joke's on me, I guess." He grimaced while fastening his seatbelt. "I shouldn't have tried to keep up with my kids like I did."

No argument there. I smiled compassionately, especially since I've been known to be just as foolhardy with my own health and physical limitations. Meanwhile, Chris and Jillian offered apologies, though unnecessary.

"You have a hot tub at the place you're staying at in Gatlinburg... right?" I asked.

"It looks like a big one from the pictures Mom showed us," said Chris, his tone brightened from a moment ago.

"I suggest you make it your best friend this evening, David," I suggested.

It brought a pained smile from him. Evelyn had pulled us back onto the main drive through Cades Cove, and although David insisted we not curtail our sightseeing plans for the day, he had no qualms about skipping a visit to the most famous landmark in the park: The John Oliver Cabin. One of my personal favorites for many years, unfortunately it sat less than a mile away from the fabled ravine that had brought the Hobbs into our lives. We've enjoyed an amazing friendship forged from trial and tragedy... but those sorrowful events have forever altered my view of this scenic homestead.

The large meadow where Allie Mae's spirit physically attacked David with intent to kill him was plainly visible as we drove by it and the Oliver cabin. The scene looked benign on this warm summer afternoon... but the same uneasiness in the air, which was also prevalent when Evelyn and I accompanied David to face Allie Mae under a full October moon at midnight, thoroughly pervaded the area.

I shivered… so did David.

"What's up with you two?" teased Jillian. Her impish expression faded when neither of us responded. Evelyn and Miriam glanced back at us, their grim looks matching David's and mine. "Sorry. I forgot this was the place."

"It's okay, sweetie," David replied, forcing a smile that was almost convincing.

"Why don't we head back to our cabin to pick up the Jeep, and Grandpa and I can help you guys settle into your chalet with a pizza and movie night?" suggested Evelyn, breaking the awkward tension inside the SUV. Chris and Jillian especially liked her idea, and the oppressive feeling that seemed to have latched onto us as we passed the Oliver place began to dissipate.

By the time we returned to my cabin, much of the jovial mood in which we started the day had returned. The late afternoon sun bathed the tall pines, and things felt as they usually did. Whatever menacing presence had paid us a visit last night remained absent... but for how long? Did it have anything to do with what we briefly experienced in the cove?

These silent questions prompted me to keep Shawn inside the cabin after we helped our guests load up their luggage in both the Jeep and the Hobbs' rented Chevy. Evelyn and I planned to return home later that night....

The chalet David and Miriam picked out was a real beauty, with a spectacular view of Gatlinburg. Since it overlooked the main part of town, pizza was just a phone call away. Evelyn used her Netflix account to pick out a couple of movies everyone could enjoy, and she and I soon had worthy distractions to keep from thinking about what might be happening elsewhere.

Galiena remained silent. Her absence from my thoughts surprised me most, since I had often sensed her close proximity when Evelyn and I would visit Gatlinburg, and the demure spirit would project her thoughts to me.

Yet, so far I felt nothing from her.

"How about John and I get a head start on the hot tub?" David suggested, when it came time for the second movie—a romantic comedy I had seen before and David stated he wasn't in the mood for. "We'll keep it warm for everyone else."

I thought for a moment Chris might want to join us, but Jillian convinced him to stick around for the flick starring a young gal he was apparently infatuated with. Evelyn had thought ahead to bring my swim trunks, and once I had changed into them I found David waving a couple of longnecks from inside the hot tub.

"Evelyn advised that she'll be driving home tonight. So, if you get a little tipsy, you'll be fine," drawled David, his boyhood twang from Chattanooga shining through. "Are you okay with shootin' the shit for a little while?"

"Sounds good." I noticed the pain I sensed yesterday in him hovered closer to the surface, lurking in his eyes.

After a few minutes of small talk about work and looking forward to watching Tyler play football on Saturdays for the same school David attended twenty-two years ago, he broached the subject I dreaded most.

"Do you ever go back to the ravine?"

"Not since we fenced the damned place off six years ago." I felt uncomfortable discussing the ravine, as if whatever was buried there would somehow perk up and listen in from afar. "I hope to never see it again."

David nodded thoughtfully. "You're probably wondering why I'm bringing it up now—sort of out of the blue."

"It does seem odd that you wouldn't want to let sleeping dogs lie—especially after what you, Miriam, and Evelyn went through," I confessed. "Even Chris, Jill, and Ty have had their dealings with—"

"Don't say her name, John!" he interrupted. "That's a promise you and I made to each other long ago that I intend to keep."

"So, you still think about what happened, huh?" I asked, gently. It seemed best to steer away from the subject of Allie Mae and also Teutates.

"Actually, not so much anymore, my friend," said David, pausing to drain nearly half of his Sam Adams. I had barely nursed mine. "What happened back then hasn't been even a fleeting thought lately... until last night. Something happened."

"Like what?" The inside of my mouth suddenly turned dry from dread. I took a healthy swallow of beer while awaiting David's response.

"I heard a woman's voice whispering outside your bedroom window," he said. "It woke me up, man. But Miriam slept right through it. The voice even called to me by my name…."

David polished off his beer and set the bottle on the deck outside the hot tub. The glistening lights from other chalets surrounded us, spread out across the valley from where we presently sat nestled in bubbling warmth. Along with the bright lights from Gatlinburg below, the area's ambiance had engendered a sense of security… until I thought about my guests last night lying in their beds while a hostile presence tested the perimeter of my home.

"And you think it was 'her' again?"

"No… actually I don't," said David. "The tone and delivery of the words were different… almost garbled like whoever it was could barely speak English. Something about the voice almost made me get up and go outside to her, John. I've never experienced anything like it."

I shrugged, determined to not let on that I likely knew who this mysterious female was… or at least had it narrowed down to two candidates.

Teutates disguised as a woman or the demoness Brigindo?

"What is it, John?" David asked, eyeing me suspiciously. "Do you know who she is?"

"I'm not entirely sure yet," I replied. "It might be Teutates awakening again."

I didn't wish to alarm him, and at the same time I worried that I should've heeded Evelyn's warning to stay the hell away from North Carolina. Had I unwittingly awakened another sleeping wicked entity—one that might soon visit harm as Teutates had done years earlier? I could tell from David's shocked expression that he wanted to discuss what in the hell I meant by Teutates being awakened once more. But I resolved to move on to other things.

Fortunately, before David could launch into the interrogation my careless comment deserved, Chris and Jillian decided to join us. They announced excitedly that the movie no longer won out against the hot tub experience, and Miriam and Evelyn would also be joining us shortly.

For the rest of the evening, the subject of Teutates and his forgotten siblings lying in a similar ravine near Cherokee remained off limits. David and I both understood this fact, and once he hoarded the rest of the longnecks in the fridge, hope of an even longer reprieve grew strong in my heart. If only Evelyn had decided to drink as well, it might've helped loosen her grip on the deepening worry I saw hovering around her aura.

My immediate worry was in regard to what might be waiting for us when we returned home later that night. I expected Shawn to be all right, protected by traditional blessings we had used since the last spiritual assault involved the cabin. But extending that protection beyond the pine-wall boundaries was another matter entirely.

That alone was enough to almost make us accept the offer of spending the night with the Hobbs clan, instead of going home and then returning to Gatlinburg the next afternoon for the Independence Day festivities…. Almost. The excuse of taking care of our aging 'pup' won out.

As we prepared to drive home, shortly before midnight, I offered a silent prayer for protection upon us all. Along with a whispered plea to Galiena to watch over Evelyn and me… or at least warn us if an unwanted guest awaited our arrival back home.

Chapter Five

Normally, if anything spooks Shawn in my absence, he barks with a shrillness that speaks to his fear. Yet, when we arrived home that night, he remained curiously quiet when we opened the door, prompting Evelyn to call for him nervously. Both of us were greatly relieved to find him lying leisurely in his bed by the fireplace. In fact, he didn't venture from his comfortable spot until ready to take care of his personal business outside, where he lingered longer than usual. He lifted his head several times to survey the yard… but without a single growl. All was peaceful and serene in the shadowed woodlands beyond the security lights' glow.

Although Shawn's behavior seemed odd, I soon took it as a positive sign, along with my own sense of peace. I sensed Galiena's presence from somewhere nearby. Even so, I expected my shy spirit guide to continue her standoffish ways until my granddaughter returned to her apartment in Knoxville. It meant another month of this détente would be in store, since Evelyn wouldn't return to college until August to finish her second master's degree, this one in anthropology. She holds a master's degree in civil engineering, which could pay her well. But she has explained that a change in what lies ahead for Mother Earth has inspired this latest direction… so I try not to question her change of heart.

"I don't feel anything tonight," she announced, after following my precautionary patrol of the inside perimeter of the cabin. I had just returned to my cherished recliner, and turned on the DVR to catch up on a true detective series I enjoy. I planned on retiring within the hour, and needed some time to wind down from the day. "How about you?"

"I think we're okay for now," I agreed.

"So, you don't think she'll be back?"

"Whom are you talking about?"

My attempt at acting coy failed miserably, as Evelyn stood in the kitchen with both hands on her hips. She was obviously irritated, and most likely with me.

"Grandpa, please don't play me like that," she said. "The entity... Brigindo? I'm fairly certain I sensed her presence last night. She can't break through the barrier, but she was outside the house."

"How would you know? Did you see her?" I was curious to learn if she sensed the hostile presence in the same manner I had, and if she could actually picture Brigindo where I could not.

"No... it was more a feeling," she said. "And, I thought I heard something... like guttural whispers."

"When was that?"

"Shortly after midnight... I think you were asleep. I saw a shadow on the backdoor window." She pointed to the door. "Did you hear anything?"

"No." I looked at her solemnly, determined to hide my thoughts.

Evelyn shook her head disgustedly.

"What is it, Grandpa? Better to tell me now, instead of leaving me to wonder what you know and are refusing to share with me."

"I didn't hear anything.... But I felt the presence of an entity." I released a low sigh. "I couldn't tell who or what was out there and still can't, to be fully honest. David said he heard a woman's voice outside the back window in my bedroom.... A woman calling his name."

"When did he tell you this?"

"Tonight... in the hot tub. It's what he wanted to discuss, I believe. But we couldn't once the kids showed up."

"So, it was Brigindo, you think?"

"Could be Abnoba for all we know," I said, wanting to keep things open until we knew for certain.

"It felt too hostile to be a tree fairy," she said, chuckling wearily.

"A forest deity known to drink the blood of human beings is now a mere sprite to you?" I retorted, paraphrasing what she had told me about this 'goddess' less than a week earlier.

"Grandpa, please!"

"Or it could be Teutates in disguise."

I would've expected her to consider this possibility seriously before now... but, apparently, she hadn't. Her eyes were suddenly fearful, and I could tell she no longer wanted to discuss *any* of what happened last night.

"Sometimes it's better to leave well enough alone, Evelyn," I said calmly, hoping she'd let the matter go. I could tell she didn't want to concede anything and likely wouldn't have, if not for the fact it was Teutates we were discussing and not some other immortal fiend. "As long as the barrier holds up, we should wait before stirring things up and possibly invite the Devil by curiosity or fear. Don't you agree?"

She didn't answer, instead repeating her inspection of the windows and doors throughout the cabin, along with mirrors and other reflective surfaces. Once satisfied we were not in any immediate danger, she came over to Shawn and lay on the floor next to him.

"Our boy will let you know if, or when, it's time to panic," I teased, though the implied message to relax remained earnest.

She responded with a tentative smile.

Thankfully, the rest of the night proved to be uneventful. After sleeping in Saturday morning, almost until noon, we dressed and then met the Hobbs' family at Dollywood in Pigeon Forge that afternoon. The July Fourth festivities were already in full swing, with a 'grand fireworks' show planned for that evening.

I glimpsed Galiena at nightfall, just before the evening's celebration was set to begin. She stood in the shadows near one of the newer amusement rides. I rose from the bench I shared with David, believing at first that she wished to communicate with me away from everyone else. I felt confident that only I could see her, as from the waist down she appeared opaque in the moonlight two days beyond full.

Galiena shook her head and motioned for me to remain with the others. Surprised by her response, at least she wasn't frowning. For her to appear in this manner, I assumed she had something pressing to share. Yet the lack of urgency brought a sense of hope, as if all would continue to be well in our world for the time being. I prayed this wasn't naiveté on my part, since the events of the past week supported a much different view, despite the immediate reprieve.

The prospects of resuming my conversations with her sometime soon appeared promising. It wouldn't happen that night, though, as confirmed by her essence fading from view. Meanwhile, Evelyn watched me as I returned to the bench, and her gaze was repeatedly drawn to the spot where I had seen Galiena. The look of intense concentration and then frustration revealed she hadn't caught the spirit's physical manifestation.

David didn't revisit our conversation from the night before. I believe his avoidance was more on account of his children's close proximity—perhaps Miriam's too. We parted ways with the intent of meeting again for brunch on Sunday, this time in Gatlinburg. Another fun-filled day was in the offing—

especially for Chris, who had anxiously waited to ride the go-carts at several locations along the strip.

But by the following morning, things had changed.

While I was outside the cabin making sure Shawn had enough food and water for the day, Evelyn suddenly screamed for me to come inside. Shawn beat me to the back door, and when I followed him to the living room, I found my granddaughter sitting on her knees with her hands over her mouth. Her gaze was fixed on the television screen perched above the fireplace mantel.

She had said earlier that she planned to check the Weather Channel to see if we needed to bring umbrellas with us that afternoon. It appeared she never made it past CNN.

"Oh my God..."

It was all I could mutter as I stared at the TV. At first, I only noticed the sheriff cruisers parked around a wooded area cordoned off with yellow crime scene tape. It could've been anywhere... or so I thought at first. But even before I heard the reporter's briefing to viewers who were just tuning in to the broadcast, I saw the North Carolina tags on two of the vehicles. Then I saw the grand log-mansion in the background, also cordoned off.

It's the ravine in Blankenship Pines!

"Grandpa... it *happened*," whispered Evelyn through her tears. "Just as I... just as I *feared... It's really bad!*"

I could've asked her what she meant, but I already knew.... A demon that had long been restrained had struck and left terrible carnage in its wake, though no one working the crime scene would ever believe it. Not in the modern world where tales about deities worshipped by the ancients are regarded entirely as fables.

The news crew's camera view panned to the curved drive to the enormous home closest to the ravine, where just days earlier I had seen three precious children at play. Two cruisers were parked next to the garage, along with a dormant ambulance and what appeared to be a coroner's sedan.

I tried to listen to the female news anchor while my heart thudded angrily.

"...For those of you just joining us, we have breaking news from Cherokee, North Carolina. Police are looking for two suspects believed to be responsible for the bludgeoning deaths of five people sometime between Friday night and early Saturday morning. The family who had recently moved into the home behind the tree line is believed to have been killed while sleeping, and police are working to determine when the attacks occurred...."

My heart broke for the family involved, and my silent anger against Simon Blankenship raged as a volatile inferno. I gently lifted Evelyn to her feet and took her into my arms, seeking to comfort her as I once did when she was a young girl, and again as an adult when she would awaken in the night screaming from terrible nightmares following her experience with Teutates.

The news anchor went on to report that the eldest daughter of four children in the family became concerned when her parents and siblings didn't return to Asheville, where they were from, Saturday afternoon. She waited for a friend to make the trip with her to the new subdivision, and made a grisly discovery shortly after midnight.

The pretty young blonde on the television suddenly became excited, talking to a male reporter at the scene while he jogged with cameras behind him to where a gentleman stood, whom I recognized from my Thursday visit to the site. Amos Johnson stood outside the construction trailer where I had watched him shuffle off to before I left that afternoon. Now, dozens of journalists and other reporters surrounded him, while the guy from CNN tried to poke a microphone in close enough to hear Mr. Johnson's response to one journalist's question.

"Well, I can't begin to imagine Joe or Pete doing something like this," he said. "No sir.... It's just terrible... The Stevens family were real nice folk. I'm so sorry for what happened...."

He couldn't finish, and I could see tears around the edges of his polarized glasses.

"What's that?" he responded to another question. "Like I told the police, our guys were laying some pipe on Friday and we had to stop when we ran into some more bedrock problems in the ground. It's all fixed now.... We got everything cleaned up around four o'clock and then Joe and Pete stayed behind to make sure things were secured for the weekend. They were gone when Steve Parker and I made it back that night. Everything was locked up as it was supposed to be, so we went on home."

Someone else asked another question, and I heard the name Simon Blankenship mentioned.

"No ma'am... you'll have to talk to him," said Amos, his tone suddenly stern. "If you'll excuse me, I need to get with those officers over there."

He pointed to where a pair of sheriff's deputies stood near one of the cruisers. The media crowd pursued him until another deputy waved them off. By then, I could no longer hear what the reporter or news anchor were saying.... Galiena's voice filled my mind instead.

"Running Deer... I'm so sorry," she said. "It's not too late to make a difference. The danger is real, and I can't promise to keep you from harm, other than I'll try. But... *please* come! My people need you.... *Your* people need you. If Brigindo and the others escape the realm of Devil Mountain, they will be next."

The weight upon my heart was heavy… but the look on Evelyn's face was worse.

Although unsure if she could discern the message delivered to my mind, my granddaughter must've picked up something from either it or the images in my head. Images of returning to North Carolina, and soon.

Sorrow turned to worry in her eyes, and then heated anger.

A moment of reckoning was about to begin.

Chapter Six

"You're *not* going back there!"

Evelyn resisted my efforts to downplay what she had gathered from my thoughts. As I feared, she received a clear picture of my latest intentions—even if the source that inspired the images remained a mystery to her. All that mattered was what she could foresee happening as a result of my further meddling in a situation that could only get worse.

"Do you want them to wage war against us?" Evelyn continued, while touching up her makeup since we were now late for our brunch date with the Hobbs clan. "We already know one of the entities has been here, Grandpa—it matters not if it was Brigindo, Abnoba, or the others. Hell, it doesn't matter if it was Teutates instead! The fact that one has escaped and has started a killing rampage means it's too late to stop it!"

I couldn't give her an immediate rebuttal—largely because she was right. The bloodshed had begun, and the wanton slaughter of the innocent I had witnessed through Searix's eyes from his *Akasha* memories now returned to the forefront of my mind.

"But what about the innocent people living in the area?" I asked, when ready to respond. "They are all sitting ducks right now—just as the family who was butchered this weekend was unaware of the ruthless threat invading their new home. These demons will never answer to our laws and morality—you know this. Not to mention the looming threat to our people—"

"Are you sure you didn't mean *her* people?" interrupted Evelyn. "How dare she go there? She's not even Cherokee!"

Oh shit. "Whom are you talking about?"

Obviously, Evelyn had picked up on Galiena's entreaty, in addition to the rest of the message. My granddaughter's disdain told me it was likely she also heard Galiena's voice inside my head.

"Grandpa... you can now take pleasure in being right about one thing. Galiena is definitely real," she said, shaking her head in annoyance as she grabbed the keys to the Jeep. I followed her out the front door, losing ground to her angry pace as I locked it. "This fact doesn't make her any better than the entities she's supposedly protecting us from—especially if she insists on you returning to North Carolina without any kind of advantage."

She climbed in the vehicle and started the engine.

"You keep forgetting that the Iroquois—Galiena's tribe—are our ancient ancestors. So, in a sense the Cherokee living on the Reservation are her people, too. When you finally see her appear to you personally, you'll know she is nothing like the others," I said, struggling to get my seatbelt on before Evelyn raced the Jeep down the driveway. "This isn't like your Nissan.... I'd prefer to keep my Jeep in tip-top shape, if you don't mind."

"Sorry... but you know how I feel about being late," she replied, her anger cooling. She offered a weak smile and I returned it. "You should probably call David to let him know we're going to be about fifteen minutes late—and maybe thirty if you don't let me gun it to get there."

"I'll call him in a moment.... I don't want to tell him or Miriam about the news. Let them bring it up."

"All right. But what if David or Miriam makes a connection between the ravines?"

"They won't… or at least I hope they won't," I sought to assure her. "But it's too late to pretend we can escape the consequences—regardless of whether or not we get involved."

Profound sorrow descended upon me—mostly for the young victims I had worried about the past few days. I knew from experience the details released by the police were tempered in comparison to what actually happened. If Brigindo was responsible for the deaths, then being bludgeoned would be merciful compared to what this entity preferred to do.

"You can't think about that sort of thing, Grandpa," said Evelyn. "Not without me being aware of it, too. Besides, unless you were there you wouldn't know for certain… speculation can be worse torture."

"Well, then, either I stay here and worry about people dying elsewhere, or go try to make a difference."

"You mean *we* can go there."

"What about our guests?"

"That depends on how you handle it, Grandpa. Either you wait until they go home, or you can get real creative with how you explain our needed absence."

"I don't think I can wait… I mean *we*," I told her, smiling weakly. "Although if I went alone, you could keep them entertained… perhaps?"

That idea wouldn't work once the news of what happened near Cherokee went viral. David and Miriam might not at first realize the similarities to Teutates' murderous rampage from six years earlier. However, if the lurid details concerning the deaths were ever made public, our friends from Colorado might well make the connection to a brutality that favored Teutates and then become too curious for their own good.

"Only if it turns out Brigindo killed the security guards, too," Evelyn advised, obviously gleaning information from my thoughts again.

"Do you mind staying out of my head?" I chided, but with enough seriousness to get her to stop.

"Only if you quit trying to change my mind," she said. "I'm going if you're going, so if you want me to stay here, then you stay too. Besides, David came here mainly to be with you—his best friend. How can you leave him again without him wondering what in the hell is so important in North Carolina for you to go back there? You don't think he'll be curious to find out why?"

She had a point—the best one yet, actually. I needed time to consider our stalemate, to see if there might be some other solution I had failed to consider that could accomplish what Evelyn said wasn't going to happen: to change her mind.

My granddaughter went for the jugular later that afternoon, while Chris and Jillian raced against each other at one of the larger go-cart tracks.

"Did either of you catch the report out of North Carolina this morning?" she asked Miriam and David, drawing a reproachful look from me that I soon regretted.

"You mean the family that was murdered near Cherokee?" asked Miriam, to which Evelyn nodded. "Horrible… what kind of monster would do something like that? The report said there were three children among the victims."

"Does it have anything to do with why you were there last week?" asked David, eyeing me suspiciously.

"Not necessarily," I said, shooting a pleading look to Evelyn to hold her tongue.

"Oh, Grandpa—these are our friends for Pete's sake!" said Evelyn, ignoring a stronger look to get her to keep quiet. "An evil man has refused to listen to our brothers and sisters from the reservation, and as a result a luxury subdivision has been erected on hallowed ground."

Miriam gasped. "It can't be happening again…."

"I'm afraid it is," said Evelyn.

Miriam moved closer to David, who wrapped his arms around her while keeping me locked in his gaze. It wasn't anger or even irritation… but he definitely seemed hurt.

Hurt by me attempting to leave him out of this to protect him and his family from harm? Seriously?

"It's the reason I was there… I tried to take care of things before y'all arrived in Tennessee," I admitted, feeling regret in having to explain my actions—made worse by the fact I failed to make a difference in North Carolina. The cherub-sweet face of the little girl playing in the ravine came to mind—a child who was now dead—inflaming my fury again. "I failed to stop the *anisginas* from doing harm… and it's best that I go alone to face them once more."

"Grandpa, talking like that is insane!" scolded Evelyn, loud enough to draw attention from other people gathered near the go-cart track.

I motioned for us all to step further away, for better privacy.

"On the contrary, talking like that is noble, since protecting those we love from harm should come first and foremost," I replied, immediately seeing the hypocrisy of my words as they left my mouth. I could feel my face flush.

"John, I told you the other night what I heard, when the woman's voice called to me," said David. "What's to stop that from happening again in your absence? We'd be just as safe with you as apart…. What is it, Babe?"

Miriam gazed intently into his face, shaking her head. "You didn't tell me about hearing anything, David," she said. "I thought I was the only one who heard something."

"I heard whispers," said Evelyn. "And Grandpa sensed an entity circling the cabin outside."

Miriam nodded slightly, her lower lip quivering.

"I'm sorry, my love," said David. "I just didn't want you or the kids worrying about anything."

"I might've also seen something," she confessed, and then paused, as if unsure what to say next.

We waited for her to go on… but we wouldn't have long. Chris and Jillian had finished their go-cart race and were preparing to leave the track.

"What did you see, Miriam?" I asked, gently.

"I… I'm not really sure," she said, finally. "It didn't seem real, but neither did Teutates when we dealt with him. I think it was a woman. Pure white skin and buck-naked…. She had a shapely slender form, but her face seemed longer than it should be… the back of her head was elongated a little, like Teutates, but her hair was different than his. She had long blonde hair… some of it worn in braids…."

"Anything else?" asked Evelyn, when Miriam hesitated again. Chris and Jillian were making their way to us.

"Her eyes," she replied. "They were lavender without pupils… beautiful but cold. Her facial features were delicate, which seemed strange to me since her lips were longer—or wider—than normal and she had to be at least seven feet in height."

"Hey, kids. Did you have fun?" David alerted us that Jillian and Chris had returned. "Who won?"

"I did, of course!" Chris was beaming.

"Dad it was a blast—you should try this one!" Jillian enthused, and then her smile and Chris's faded. "What's up with everyone? You're acting like someone died." She laughed nervously.

"Sorry sweetie," said David, reaching for his wallet and handing her a pair of twenties. "How about you and Chris go over to that concession stand and get us all some funnel cakes?"

It proved to be an effective distraction. We waited until the pair was out of earshot to say anything else.

"You should allow us to join you, John," said David.

"What about the kids?" I asked.

"We'll make sure they stay out of harm's way—somehow," promised Miriam.

The three of them watched me expectantly. Even though each had presented a case for coming along, I wasn't convinced it was a wise choice. In fact, nothing Evelyn, David, or Miriam could've said or done would make me feel the risk of being torn apart by four entities the modern world has never seen the likes of—except those unfortunate to deal with Teutates—would be worth accompanying me back to Cherokee. But Evelyn had already made it a 'twosome' I couldn't renege.

"It might be best if you return to Colorado now, and let Evelyn and me make it up to you in some way," I said, drawing an exasperated sigh from my granddaughter while David and Miriam continued to give me their undivided, stone-faced attention. "We can come see you in October, when Evelyn has her fall break from school. And, you already know my schedule is wide open until the Great Spirit calls me home." I added what I hoped was a charming smile…. It mattered little since my pitch failed miserably.

David intended on coming along, pointing out as part owner of his CPA firm he could set his own hours and vacation time due to the long hours he had put in for two consecutive tax seasons.

Extending a vacation was even easier for Miriam, since she was already moving toward retirement from the clinic she co-founded. Her partners were already handling the bulk of the day-to-day running of the business. She had reduced her clientele down to a handful of children whose parents were insistent on seeing only her for their medical needs. Fortunately, she only had one summer appointment scheduled from this group, and it wasn't until the fifth of August. Emergencies were routinely handled by the staff on hand, as had been the Littleton Children's Clinic's policy since its inception nearly ten years ago.

"I am badly outnumbered," I said, to which they all chuckled. Too bad my comment wasn't intended to be funny. "What about Chris and Jill?"

A glance toward the line they stood in confirmed they had yet to be served.

"Well we can't leave them here, Grandpa."

"I know, Evelyn… just making a point," I said.

"They could stay at the hotel we end up booking," suggested Miriam. "We can make sure they have plenty to do in the way of fun… make sure the hotel has a pool. Then at night—or whenever we're not working on this situation— David and I can take them around to see the sights."

"There are lots of fun things to do in Cherokee," added Evelyn, seemingly forgetting for the moment how much fun it might be if Brigindo or Smetrios decided to crash the party.

I wished right then that Galiena could somehow show Evelyn the images given to me when Searix's memories were impressed upon my mind. It might change her tune considerably about what 'fun' meant to these demons when slaughtering people—including children—for food and sport. Our location in a fairly busy and populated metropolis would be a limited deterrent to what these entities might do. After all, a crowd of people to them wouldn't be much different than the ancient pilgrimages among the Gallic peoples, who brought offerings and gathered in the thousands to annually worship these wicked beings, prior to the Roman invasion ending it all.

"You will tell the kids what we're up against?" I asked.

"Do you really think it's necessary to spell it all out, Grandpa—or even the best idea?" Evelyn responded.

"Yes, I do," I told her. "Brigindo took offense to my presence in Blankenship Pines the other day, and it appears she followed me all the way back home. What do you suppose will happen the next time she's less than thrilled by our presence?"

She had no answer for this. Neither did David and Miriam.

"Just promise me that at the very first sign of trouble, the four of you will hop on an airplane and head back to Littleton," I said. "Otherwise there's no deal, and you can either stay here and enjoy the rest of your stay without us, or head home—the wisest choice. Agreed?"

David and Miriam didn't need to consult with each other, offering confident affirmations just as their children gathered the treats and were on their way back to where we waited. Like a good-looking Hansel and Gretel as young adults, and just as unaware of the hungry witch that awaited them… awaited us all.

Chapter Seven

We tried to handle things in the right way on Monday, with the intent of obeying the laws of North Carolina. Dealing with a supernatural adversary could only be made worse if the local police and the Swain County Sheriff's Department were also unhappy with our presence.

It meant a return trip to Blankenship Enterprises, unfortunately, to seek the owner's blessing in regard to our aspirations. In the end, I should've saved us the trouble. Evelyn would have also foregone the attempt to sway a pigheaded man as hell bent as Simon Blankenship, but only if we hadn't needed a damned good reason to take matters into our own hands.

"The answer is going to be the same, Mr. Running Deer," Julie Persinger advised, soon after Evelyn, Miriam, David, and I stepped inside the office. I was impressed she remembered my name, though it could be just as much a bad thing as a positive omen. "Mr. Blankenship is a very busy man, and doesn't have time for any of your Indian concerns. That's why he referred you to our attorney."

"Yes, and I thank you for the referral, as we may pursue that course if something can't be done here. But all we are asking for is a supervised visit to Blankenship Pines," I explained. "There will be no protests set up or anything else to interrupt the work going on there. And, I can give Mr. Blankenship our signed promise to not pursue anything with our Native American brethren here in North Carolina—or anywhere else, for that matter."

My specific desire was to see the ravine and confirm its condition in person. Obviously, work had continued after my visit, and I was especially worried by Amos Johnson's response to the media about 'cleaning things up' after encountering more digging problems on Friday. Had the ossuary that lay exposed on Thursday been further damaged or removed? It could help explain the escalation to violence that followed on Saturday.

Of worse concern was the status of the other three ossuaries that remained buried in the ground when I previously surveyed the ravine. What we would soon face could be worsened tremendously if it was more than Brigindo that had escaped, and we were forced to deal with multiple entities on the loose.

It's important to keep in mind that the bloody rampages of these creatures throughout their history coincided with taking on flesh again, moving from the world of spirit to our reality as physical beings. We had seen this played out during Teutates' brief reign of terror, and he had almost become unstoppable when his physical manifestation was on the cusp of being fully realized. Not to mention, I had also witnessed the phenomena played out through Searix's eyes in ancient Germania.

Galiena, who had been silent in my previous trip to Cherokee, surprised me with a visit on the way to North Carolina that morning. Evelyn and I had brought the Jeep while the Hobbs traveled in their rented Chevrolet. Evelyn drove for us after a restless night's sleep for me, and as we followed David I found it harder and harder to keep my eyes open.

Maybe the only way Galiena could reach me in our neighboring state was through dreams. Regardless, it was my most lucid experience with her since before the holiday weekend.

"Hello, Running Deer." She was driving the Jeep instead of Evelyn, which only mildly surprised me since 'strangeness' is often the status quo when dealing with her in dreamscapes. "I fear you won't have long to stop Brigindo from waking the others."

"Do you mean that their ossuaries remain intact? Or, is it too late already?" I tried to intuitively picture the present state of the ravine.

"I don't know... I have not been able to return there since last time," she said, removing her gaze from the road ahead to study me. Her eyes were a deeper blue than I recalled ever seeing before... such profound sadness! "I can sense things still... but the only way I can see anything in Cherokee is for you to 'become' my new eyes. What you see will be my only view of the ravine, and the only way to tell if the other tombs are still sealed beneath the earth's surface. Make sure you return to where you saw Brigindo's broken ossuary. From that spot, the other three will be less than fifty feet away to the north, east, and south."

"Does this also mean you can no longer pay attention to the road ahead?" I asked, suddenly aware the car was swerving. I worried we would crash into a guardrail and plunge over it to certain death... for me anyway.

"This is a dream, and you can't die... not this time," she said, smiling slightly. "Fear will be your enemy just as much as Brigindo and her siblings. Focus on staying calm at all times, and I will guide you. *Believe*, Running Deer.... There, that's better. Now look."

She pointed ahead of us. Instead of weaving as we were, the Jeep hugged the road, and the hairpin turns came smoothly despite the fact the car sped up.

"Picture calmness despite the chaos, my friend. Otherwise, you will be on your own, and I won't be able to reach you," Galiena advised. "My heart tells me that Brigindo is gaining strength, and I fear more brutally violated bodies will soon be found. If so, she will have almost completed her physical transformation. Once she reaches that state, she will have enough strength to release at least one of the others and maybe more. A greater advent of bloodshed will soon follow…."

"Grandpa, does it matter where we park?"

Evelyn's voice from the driver's seat jolted me awake, and I was surprised to discover we had reached Blankenship Enterprises. David parked the Chevy next to us, where Jillian and Chris would wait for his and Miriam's return. If for some miracle Simon Blankenship agreed to let us view the ravine that day, the plan was for Miriam to take the kids to the Fairview Inn where we had reserved two suites across from each other, and then David would join Evelyn and me to visit the site….

"It's okay, Julie… send 'em on back here, and we'll talk."

Blankenship stood in the doorway to his personal office, and though the main entrance and lobby were modest in furnishings, I could already tell it wasn't the case for the big boss's abode. Ms. Persinger bristled with the displeasure of a bobcat covered in fire ants, ushering us into the plush environment that normally protected her employer from the likes of my companions and me.

"Mr. Running Deer?" he said, after we all stepped inside and he shut the door behind us.

"Call me John," I replied, to which he nodded as if amused, though the annoyance in his light blue eyes clearly announced he wasn't.

Simon Blankenship would be considered quite handsome if looks alone were considered the defining qualities of a desirable man. His thick, light brown hair was brushed back in a dovetail that would've been popular when I was a teenager, revealing the hair color as a camouflage to make his mid-sixty-ish appearance much closer to late-forties. Despite sporting a deep tan, his face lacked any deep lines and other telltale aging signs—surely a cosmetic benefit afforded by the man's wealth.

He sized me up, and though he was a few inches shorter than David or me, I got the feeling he wondered how hard it would be to take us on physically. Very strange, but the sensation of overt hostility was unmistakable. It surprised me even more that he had invited us back into his private chamber for a chat. No doubt he planned for it to be short and sweet, heaviest on the former.

"Okay, Mr. Running Deer… I see you brought your friends with you, but nothing's changed since the message I left you last week." He folded his arms across his chest as if to reinforce the barrier of his words. "Julie's right… I really don't have time for this bullshit. But I tell you what…. I'm going to share a couple of things with you, and then I expect for you and your little merry band here to take a hike."

He eyed us all angrily, and of course I was the main focus of his ire. Finding it fairly easy to remain calm, since his fragile composure indicated some intimidation by our presence, I nodded my acceptance of his terms.

"It will undoubtedly please you to know that our operation in the Pines is on hold until August, since murder is bad for business. But also know this…. Waiting a month to resume operations should give the local authorities and the FBI—who will be here later today—enough time to complete their investigations, and get a lead on where Peter Hundley and Joe Swanson have disappeared. By my guess, those assholes are probably either halfway to Canada or somewhere down in Mexico as we speak. But they'll soon be caught, and we'll take care of the girl who lost her family. Then guess what we're gonna do next?"

He eyed me expectantly, wearing a shit-eating grin.

"I suppose this is where you want audience participation," I said, feeling Evelyn's spirit flinch nearby.

"That'd be nice," he said, snickering coldly. "But since you can't do a goddamn thing about our plans one way or another, I'll just tell y'all flat out what's coming. We're going to double our efforts to get all of the homes ready, sold, and occupied by September. I don't care what y'all are planning to do to fuck things up for us, but damned straight the work will be done by mid-August at the latest. So, again—and for the *very last time*—if you've got a problem with *anything* I've said, contact my lawyer. You already have his name and number."

"David Lavine," I said, to which he nodded. "Does this mean you aren't willing to supervise a visit inside the development? We promise to not enlist another Indian group to cause you any more grief. All we want is a look inside, and regardless of what we find, we will leave and not come back, and all of us will stay out of your hair forever."

A grand promise that could prove impossible to keep. But delivering a slight dishonesty to a loathsome character that wouldn't know integrity and honor if either one bit him on the ass was worth the chance. For a moment, it looked like he actually considered the idea. But then he shook his head and pointed to the door.

"Get the hell out of my office, Mr. Running Deer!" he snarled. "I'd better never lay eyes on your sorry ass and your pals ever again—you hear me? And, don't even think about visiting the Pines. I'll have all of your asses thrown in jail! Now, go on... get the hell out of here!"

I ignored the smug looks from Julie Persinger and her two assistants as the four of us exited the building, all the while focusing on Galiena's admonitions from my dream.

"Well, I'd say that went really well," David dryly observed, once outside. "What do we do now?"

"I'm not sure, yet…. But the next step will come to me," I said, after a wistful shrug.

"Why did you even bother asking him to chaperone us, Grandpa? Now Blankenship knows our intentions and will be ready to stop us!" Evelyn was visibly upset, surely believing I had killed our chances of sneaking into the development unnoticed. Perhaps she was right….

"We needed an olive branch before throwing down a gauntlet," I advised. "It would've been worse had we not tried to reason with Blankenship first. Getting caught sneaking into the ravine would be worse if we had blatantly bypassed seeking his permission."

"That makes no sense!" Evelyn seethed. "We'll go to jail just the same if we get caught!"

"True," I admitted. "Our chances of going to jail are just the same."

I could almost hear my grandfather telling me from the place he rests in peace that the noble thing was to come in amity first…. And now I would at least have the blessing of my forefathers to invade sacred land that has never belonged to Simon Blankenship as it was. All of *Tsvsgina Odalv*—Devil Mountain—have long belonged to the four entities buried in its shadow. That fact was undisputable regardless of what my ancestors believed was their land, and would remain just as valid in the present day despite Blankenship's claims of ownership. No human could lay claim to any of the acreage as long as the deities from ancient Gaul held sway.

"My heart tells me the demons will remain an increasingly terrible force to reckon with, and can only be vanquished according to the laws of the spirit world where their realm is based," I continued, hoping my granddaughter's heart, as well as David's and Miriam's, would recognize the wisdom. "Doing things the right way without fear of the consequences is the only approach to take… even if the initial steps look incredibly naïve or foolish."

Unsure how effectively I explained my reasoning, I braced for a possible stronger rebuke from Evelyn. But to my surprise, and relief, her exasperation melted into something much more pliable. Without saying another word, she nodded thoughtfully.

"You know I respect you immensely, John… but I have to admit I am confused about how we're supposed to stop what's going on here," said David, once we reached where our vehicles were parked. "Are we still going to the ravine today—despite what that asshole threatened to do? Or, do we have a Plan B?"

"It might be better to wait until after dark to try anything," I said. "But I intend to visit the ravine as soon as reasonably possible."

"Day or night, it sounds like a great way to get shot," said Evelyn. "Or worse, if Brigindo is waiting to greet us with open arms…. Maybe we should go check into our rooms, grab a bite, and talk about it some more."

"The Plan B part," David added teasingly.

Miriam cleared her throat to get our attention. "John, my biggest concern is this…. If you verify the bones are either there or gone, what will that tell you?" She shivered despite the mid-nineties temperature, while nervously looking over her shoulder as if an invisible presence had just now approached from behind her. "Regardless if it is one entity escaped from its tomb or all of them, I still don't see how we can keep them from attacking someone—and likely getting ourselves killed"

A great point, and the very thing I had thought about most since discovering Brigindo's bones protruding from her tomb last Thursday afternoon. Worse, I didn't have an answer yet. Just a feeling the right solution would come if I remained patient and kept my eyes and heart open.

"I believe Evelyn is right," I said, drawing curious looks from them all, as the kids rolled down the Chevrolet's windows to find out the latest news.

"How so, Grandpa? You just got done defending your decision to come here."

"And it was indeed the right decision, Evelyn," I told her, smiling weakly. "I'm talking about your other point and David's. Let's go get settled, fill our stomachs, and hone in on the details for an effective Plan B. Regardless of what we don't know yet, it all begins in the ravine. Before the night's over, we will either find a way inside or face the consequences for trying."

Chapter Eight

Getting settled in at the hotel, along with a decent meal, did help lift the spirits of everyone. The mood continued to improve as we familiarized ourselves with the most popular points of interest in Cherokee, and not just the casinos. However, by nightfall—and after we had spent the better part of an hour discussing the available options to accomplish what we came for—'Plan B' began to look a lot like 'Plan A'.

Our most viable choice was to take our chances by visiting Blankenship Pines at night, hoping we might slide past any police or security surveillance by arriving after dark. In other words, we'd be living on a wing and a prayer… the four adults, that is. Jillian and Chris would stay behind, agreeing to not leave the three-bedroom suite they shared with their parents.

The kids seemed content with the idea of movies and video games to tide them over until our return from the ravine. But to be safe, Evelyn set up a boundary using the Cherokee herbs and roots she brought with her, along with the protective incantations most suitable for this situation, to ensure nothing with evil intent could enter the Hobbs' suite. She blessed us as well, although I worried it might not help us as much since we would soon be invading the domain of Brigindo and her siblings. Once everything was set, and we had taken care of the shovels, ropes, and anything else we might need—including back-up batteries for each of our flashlights—we set out for the north of town and Devil Mountain.

Twilight faded into moonlit dimness as we drove deeper into the mountains, steadily distancing ourselves from the warmer city lights of Cherokee.

"I can already feel it... can any of you?" asked Miriam from the backseat she shared with Evelyn. David drove and I served as his co-pilot—as much for company as being the only one of us to ever venture this far north of town. *Tsvsgina Odalv* sat in a midst of blue hills just beyond the northern border of the Eastern Cherokee Reservation. I wondered how the mountain and the unholy ravine far below its majestic eminence would look under a moon four days past its fullness.

"I'm not sure," said David. "I don't want it to merely be something I'm feeding by thinking about it."

"I can feel it, too," said Evelyn, reaching over to pat Miriam's arm. "We're going to be okay... we just need to stick together."

"How about you, John?" asked David, as we rounded the bend to where in daylight hours we would enjoy a clear view of Devil Mountain. "What do you think or feel?"

"I think it's the anticipation of where we're going... mostly," I said.

Although I couldn't see or hear her yet, I could feel Galiena's presence... she was near. Unfortunately, I could also sense a hostile presence that grew stronger with every mile marker we passed on the way to the exit that would take us to Blankenship Pines.

"What will we do if Brigindo is waiting for us, Grandpa?"

Evelyn leaned toward me from behind, as if she suddenly desired a private conversation concerning this ancient deity.

"You already know she will be," I replied, turning to face her while Miriam looked on with frightened eyes. I could feel David's deepening concern, too, but he had the distraction of driving. "The better question is whether she will be there in

78

spirit, or in the flesh—and, whether she will wish to engage us, or merely shoo us off?"

"What about Galiena?" she asked.

"Who's that?" David glanced at me before returning his sole attention to the winding highway. He and Miriam were unaware of my spirit guide, since the focus of our conversations had been on things they would readily understand—namely the demon that had likely murdered a family of five. Talking about my first serious 'advisor' from the spirit world would engender distracting questions that had little to do with our current situation.

"A friend on the other side of the veil," I said. "She once was my grandfather's guide, and has taken an interest in my personal affairs."

"It's much more than that," Evelyn corrected me. "Galiena is the reason Grandpa got involved in this mess. She apparently lived in the time when Teutates and his brothers and sisters were transported to America from Europe, and is the daughter of the German man who spearheaded the trip to dump his people's troublesome gods and goddesses in our backyard. He married an Iroquois woman, and Galiena was their only child, killed during a raid by an enemy tribe…. Have I got it right so far, Grandpa?"

"That sounds so sad… to die so young," said Miriam, echoed by David and not the reaction Evelyn expected, I'm sure.

"You make her sound like a meddling wraith, Evelyn. You're forgetting that even though Galiena reached out to me for help in keeping Teutates' siblings quarantined here in North Carolina, she also knew you and I would eventually be faced with the challenge of keeping Teutates from rising again in Tennessee," I said, mainly for David and Miriam's benefit, since the soft rebuke to my granddaughter—who is rarely this surly—could be wasted words. Evelyn had heard this explanation before and it obviously hadn't sunk in far. "Galiena is compassionate and very brave, since her spirit could have followed her tribe in their eventual migration back to the northeast. She sensed the four entities imprisoned in the ravine not far from where she was killed, biding their time to return to the land of the living. She selflessly set out to guard the ravine where the entities laid buried for more than a thousand years—as we've already discussed."

Nothing more was said until we reached our exit.

"Do you think Galiena can actually help us, John?" David asked.

We had entered the frontage road leading to Blankenship Pines, where thick darkness suddenly surrounded us, as if the moon and stars had been blotted out. I realized then we hadn't seen Devil Mountain from the highway, as I had my previous two trips during daylight hours. Only the road and whatever else stole the headlight's glow was visible.

"I hope so, David." I closed my eyes to try and hang on to Galiena's mental touch, which was becoming weaker.

The oppressive feeling that had been getting increasingly worse became much more palpable as we approached the neighborhood entrance, and I feared my guide might get stymied again. Our presence was known to someone, and likely by Brigindo, and perhaps her brothers and sister knew we were near too. I doubted the feeling of danger came from police or new security guards waiting in the darkness for us to show up… but we drove through the main gates cautiously just the same. Evelyn remarked her surprise that the gates were still open, and I found it odd as well. But it didn't necessarily mean someone had carelessly left them that way. Our unholy hostess may have provided the invitation to enter without us having to park along the frontage road and hike into the development, which we had planned for.

I hope you can see clearly through my eyes, Galiena... we are headed into hell....

"Where did the moonlight go?" asked Evelyn, worriedly.

"And the stars." David rolled down his window to peer up into the sky. Humid air poured into the vehicle, accompanied by an orchestra of crickets, tree frogs, and cicadas. "Must be some very dark clouds above... it smells like rain." He rolled the window back up, ending the concert.

"Rain wasn't in the forecast," advised Evelyn. "That could really suck."

We crept past the first guard trailer, and the wide eyes surrounding me inside our vehicle revealed that everyone was quite apprehensive as we made our ascent deeper into the vacant subdivision. We were trespassing in every sense of the word, and the feeling of being watched grew worse as we traveled the quarter mile to reach the ravine.

"I hope we're doing the right thing," whispered Miriam, surely wondering about the same things as David and Evelyn, and perhaps also considering her hellish experience when strapped to Teutates' altar. The monster ravaged her mind with a level of personal violation that took years to get over. How much worse could it be if in the clutches of Brigindo, or one of the others?

"Remember, Miriam, to stay close to David, Grandpa, and me," Evelyn advised, compassionately. "I hear your panicked thoughts to leave. Let them go, as it will do no good to turn and run. Everything we do from here on out, we need to do as a group... to stick together. Brigindo will try to separate us— don't let it happen. If nothing else, *don't* let that happen, as otherwise she will pick us apart like a lioness marking gazelles…. When it's time to leave, we must do so as 'one'. Okay?"

I detected Miriam nodding slightly in the dimness. Meanwhile, David slowed the vehicle, pointing to the yellow police tape still cordoning off the area where I had parked the previous week. The tape crisscrossed the ravine before moving up the side of the small hillside to the murdered family's stately home.

"I wonder why the police have so much of the area blocked off like this, and yet no one is here guarding the place?" said David, shaking his head.

"It's very odd," I agreed. "There should be guards, since it looks like they might've found something else unexpected."

"The 'unexpected' part makes sense, Grandpa, and we won't want to linger here for long," said Evelyn.

"We're just looking for a tomb belonging to Brigindo, right?" asked David, sounding increasingly nervous.

"We'll want to primarily take care of that task, and see if the other three ossuaries are exposed as well," I replied, thinking about my most recent dream with Galiena, and her instructions to verify the other tombs. "After that, we can leave."

Sounded simple, even though dangerous… and certainly foolhardy.

Like everyone else, I began having second thoughts about us being there. If Brigindo had escaped, we were vulnerable against an adversary who knew the area quite well—far better than we ever could. Yet, the oppressive feeling that things would only get worse if we failed to stop the escape of the other three *anisginas* spurred me on. We had to find a way to contain *all* of them.

Don't let us down, Galiena! Hear me and watch over us!

David parked as close as he could to the ravine, by my guess a little over one hundred feet away. A pair of large graders and a tractor prevented us from parking any closer.

"Okay... like Evelyn said, let's stick together." said David, taking Miriam's hand in his once outside the rental. All three waited for me to lead the way.

Admittedly, it took all of my determination to carry out the task mandated by Galiena. Increasingly worried about my companions' safety, danger lurked heavily in the air, along with the feeling of being intently studied from every angle. The combination threatened to become a distraction too difficult to ignore.

Miriam clung to David, who looked at me with imploring eyes in the soft glow from a lantern he brought along. *He is counting on me to save him and Miriam... yet I warned him not to come!* Meanwhile, everyone's flashlight beams crossed one another as we surveyed the area ahead.

"Follow me to the slight rise over here." I pointed to the area I recognized from the past Thursday. By my remembered calculations, the violated tomb should be less than fifty feet directly ahead. Despite the strong illumination from our flashlights, stepping down into the ravine meant new dangers aside from the ones we had prepared for. Water moccasins, copperheads, and coral snakes had long been a problem in the region, and would be difficult to detect at night. "Watch where you walk and try to step where I step."

A barn owl's call from the tall pines around us startled David, and he almost knocked Miriam and Evelyn into the tiny stream that flowed through the ravine's basin. Miriam and Evelyn teased him about it, and all three laughed nervously while I listened.... A sudden crack resounded from the other end of the ravine, but didn't repeat. Cautiously I continued toward the spot where I had seen the shattered lid to what I believed was Brigindo's tomb. I felt momentary relief when I found it, though the respite was short lived.

My flashlight's beam grazed the lip of the ossuary box, the white stone peering out from a hole in the ground. Resting next to it was a large cement pipe. The box had been moved since my last visit, and I didn't recall seeing the pipe before. Perhaps this was where the crew stopped Friday.

"The tomb is over here," I announced to the others.

"It's in worse shape than when you were last here," worried Evelyn, once she witnessed the same gaping hole that had since been enlarged. I could feel her uneasiness rising…. She also remarked about the pictograms and other writing along the side of ossuary… they were indeed quite similar to what we had seen in Teutates' temple in Cades Cove. "There were bones sticking out of the hole in the pictures you showed to us. I don't see any bones here… do you?"

"No," I confirmed. Although it remained a slight possibility that an unscrupulous human had removed them, I knew in my heart it wasn't the case. Brigindo had taken them. Vampiric in nature, surely she was feeding herself with blood, and intent on procuring enough to aid her latest incarnation attempt. Peering inside the broken ossuary from above confirmed the box sat empty. We were too late.

"What's this?" Miriam bent down as she reached into the void tomb and pulled out a musty smelling cloth garment covered in dirt and grime—likely the only leftovers from when the bones were removed.

"It looks like a burial shroud," said Evelyn, helping her gently lift and unfold it. "Part of it has been eaten away over the years."

"You're not thinking of taking it out of here, are you?" David asked, and I could see the wheels turning in his mind. I picked up images of Teutates from David's mind—mainly the terrible events that transpired after unearthing the demon's remains from Cades Cove and the mischief that immediately ensued at the University of Tennessee, where the remains were taken and stored… until the monster came to life.

"I don't know that we will or not," Evelyn advised. "Maybe the shroud will come in handy… or maybe we should just leave it.…"

The sound of footsteps approached, crunching pine needles echoing across the ravine from near the driveway of the murdered family. Someone was on the way to greet us. But when our flashlight beams flooded the area there was no one visible. The footsteps stopped.

"Who goes there?" David called out gruffly. "Show yourself!"

Suddenly more footsteps resounded to our left, and my flashlight's beam arrived first. Too late to see who had been there an instant ago, I caught a glimpse of something white… a blurred image of an entity, perhaps?

"Shit! Grandpa, what was that?" Evelyn was losing her nerve, and I caught images from her thoughts that were similar to David's.

"I don't know," I replied, hating the stress in my tone. "Galiena will have to forgive us for not staying any longer."

Crackling pine needles from behind us continued back across the ravine and to the house, as if a world-class runner was in a hurry to reach the darkened log mansion. Someone very tall and slightly luminescent stood in the shadows by the driveway, awash in moonlight not allowed to reach us.

"Oh my God, it's her, isn't it?" whispered Miriam in panic.

"We have to go!" I urged, no longer worried about being quiet. Whoever this entity was could hear our softest comments just as easily, and our thoughts were surely an open book as

well. "Everyone move back carefully and quickly to the car—
now!"

We were in terrible danger, and at that moment I bore as
much anger toward Galiena as I did the murderous entity
standing near the birthplace of her latest crimes. Galiena had
let us fall into a predicament we were ill prepared to handle,
and now the only rational thing left was to flee. I pictured all of
us dead, torn apart to feed Brigindo or douse the bones of her
siblings with our warm blood—despite the spiritual protection
invoked earlier by Evelyn.

The sound of crunching footfalls—both from us scurrying
out of the now dangerous basin and the entity having fun
frightening us—followed us until we reached the pavement and
raced around the construction equipment to reach the Chevy.
At that point only our footsteps resounded, and I worriedly
glanced behind us—as did the others. The darkness had again
become impenetrable, swallowing up the brief luminance from
the moon. The massive cabin overlooking the ravine was once
more invisible—as was everything else. The only thing
perceptible to our eyes was what lay ahead… the sanctuary
inside the Traverse that we'd reach in the next five to ten
seconds.

Hopefully we could climb in safely and get the hell out of
there before the thing fully perceptible to our inner senses
caught up. I felt its pursuit gaining on us, though noiseless, as
if drifting through the air like a ghost.

"I've got the doors unlocked, everyone—so jump in and
shut 'em tight!" David yelled, after pointing the remote switch
at the vehicle when we were within thirty feet.

The Chevy's unlock signal echoed eerily through the air,
and the headlights' brief flash seemed much brighter than it
had previously. David dragged Miriam behind him, sprinting to
a finish line with more urgency than I doubt he had possessed

since his college football days. Meanwhile, she still clutched the nasty shroud from Brigindo's tomb—likely out of fear and perhaps scarcely aware she had wadded it up and held it as if her life depended on protecting it.

A sinking feeling fell upon me... disaster was about to happen.

"Miriam, drop the shroud!" I shouted.

"No, Miriam—*don't* listen to him!" Evelyn cried out. *"Don't—"*

A loud thud resounded ahead of us, and Evelyn almost lost her balance after nearly running into me. Something had landed with incredible force on top of the vehicle, crumpling part of the roof. For a moment, we could see nothing. But as a predatory hiss filled the air in front of us, our unsteady hands trained enough illumination from our flashlights to reveal the creature regarding us with hungry malice from atop the Hobbs' rental.

Brigindo?

It had to be her—based on what Evelyn had researched the past few weeks. And if not, the looming figure certainly qualified as one of the four ancient deities. Pupil-less lavender eyes glowed preternaturally in the collective glow bathing the naked female... a garishly beautiful woman almost seven feet in height. Long blonde hair, partially braided, framed her face that was a curious mixture of delicate and strong features. Alabaster white sleekness in the nose and cheekbones fit in well with the shapely curves and graceful musculature. But the mouth's fullness was all wrong.... Perhaps if the lips were relaxed, I wouldn't have begun considering an alternate escape route.

The lips were pulled back in an unnatural smile, revealing twin rows of sharp, pointed teeth—not unlike a shark or piranha. Worse, the teeth were stained by blood.... Blood that had once been a stream, now crusted, traversed down the chin, throat, and breasts of this thing almost human, but obviously not when in its predatory state.

The creature hissed again—much louder this time—and crouched as if preparing to leap to where we were all poised to flee. It seemed impossible to escape without one of us paying dearly for the decision to come here.

"Miriam... hand me the shroud," said Evelyn, softly and without removing her eyes from this thing that now turned its attention to her completely. "Hurry!"

With trembling hands, Miriam handed the shroud to Evelyn, who unraveled it as she held it out before her.

"We've come in peace, Brigindo," she said. "Let us correct the sins of those who have desecrated this holy place."

Evelyn stepped forward holding the tattered shroud out before her, while I debated tackling my granddaughter from behind and thrusting myself in front of her in sacrifice. I had absolutely no doubt Evelyn would be taken from me within the next minute—and might even be devoured despite my offering to die in her place. But before I could make a move, the creature—this likely goddess from ancient times—narrowed its eyes at Evelyn and let out a near-deafening, bone-chilling shriek.

I believed this would be it and that our lives would end within the next minute at most. However, instead, the entity leapt high into the air and landed somewhere out of earshot. Then silence followed, along with an eerie feeling of being completely alone. Brigindo—as I believe Evelyn had correctly labeled her—was gone.

The four of us scrambled into the Chevrolet, and wept in relief that we were still among the living. We'd left Blankenship Pines before Evelyn realized she was still clinging to the shroud, as Miriam had earlier. Since it seemed like a potentially regrettable idea to discard the damned thing randomly, we reluctantly took it home. If it were to be returned to the ravine, it would never happen at night. The deep dents in the Chevy's roof took care of that temptation.

While we sped back to the highway that would return us to the hotel, David worried about what he might say to the rental agency when returning the vehicle at the end of their stay. It might've been the subject to dominate our conversation, if Miriam hadn't pointed to the hills behind us. Devil Mountain stood tall, bathed in moonlight amongst its smaller brothers— just as it should've been from the moment we first arrived.

It provided a stark reminder as we hurried south to Cherokee… to keep our guard up at all times, and hopefully avoid any further confrontations with a demon-goddess on the loose.

Chapter Nine

Sleep came sparingly that night.

Not just for the four of us, but also for Chris and Jillian— and not merely from what we told them about what had happened inside Blankenship Pines. At Miriam's insistence, we avoided that subject upon our return to the hotel, speaking in generalities that we had failed to secure the site. The truth in a stretched version was better than the cold hard facts—mostly because none of us fully understood what Brigindo was capable of doing. Even with my prior knowledge from Galiena's access to the *Akasha* records concerning her father's life and memories, it was difficult to define what an unrestrained Gallic deity would do with her newfound freedom after more than ten centuries spent restrained in a virtual prison.

Even Galiena seemed at a loss, based on the thoughts that finally reached my mind as we reached Cherokee's city limits. I could feel the sadness that preceded her voice inside my head....

"We failed... I'm sorry," I told her.

"Brigindo is too strong.... She has killed four others since your return to the area this morning, and if not them, it would have been the four of you," she said. *"Two she had held as prisoners, and slaughtered less than an hour before you, Evelyn, and your friends arrived.... I sensed her surprise that you came back, Running Deer, but I couldn't warn you of the changes... HER changes and how dangerous she is now. Damn Abellio for pushing me away!"*

"Has he escaped, too?"

"No... not yet. But soon. All of them, soon."

I pictured the ravine and the impenetrable darkness. How in the hell could anyone find anything, unless purely by chance?

"I don't know!" she replied to my unvoiced question, her tone filled with sorrow and frustration. "But you must find a way to prevent Abellio and the others from joining Brigindo. You must...."

"Galiena?"

But it was the end of her contact with me that night. Surprised she was gone so abruptly, the conversation happened in an area where I had felt her presence the strongest until we were cut off.

Was it Abellio's determined reach, perhaps? Or, had Brigindo exercised her burgeoning power? Either possibility was worrisome.

Afraid to share Galiena's incomplete message with the others, I stayed with the facts from earlier that night as a guiding rule in determining what course of action to pursue next. No way in hell were we returning to the ravine without something new to work with. Something that gave us a damned good reason to be there.... It had to offer a significant advantage over Brigindo, as well as protect us from Simon Blankenship.

"So, are we going to be stuck in here again tomorrow?" Jillian asked, when all six of us gathered in the common area in Evelyn's and my suite. Evelyn and Miriam had fixed cocoa for everyone—despite the summer heat. Something about it helping us all get some badly needed rest that night. Frankly, I would try anything to not think long about Brigindo, whose bleach-white alabaster skin rekindled unpleasant memories of her brother, Teutates.

"I'm afraid so, sweetie," said David. "But it won't be until after lunch… isn't that right Evelyn? Don't we have a meeting in the afternoon with the friend you mentioned from the local university?"

"It's actually in Cullowhee, about thirty minutes from here. I'll have to first speak with Carmen, who once served as the director for Western Carolina University's Cherokee Center," Evelyn advised. "Whenever she can fit us in will be fine, and I'm assuming afternoon might be better for her. The kids can come along." She smiled at Jillian and Chris. "All we'll be doing is getting Carmen's contacts here in the state, and see if we can permanently shut down Simon Blankenship's desecration of hallowed ground."

Carmen Rainwater had been a childhood friend of Evelyn's when my daughter, Joanna, resided in Wilmington, North Carolina with Evelyn and Hanna. The kids' middle-school years were spent there, until Joanna fell for a sailor who liked to hit women. Thankfully, she allowed Evelyn and Hanna to move back to Tennessee to live with Susanne and me. We rarely heard from Joanna after that… not even when Susanne clung to a tender thread of life while dying from cancer.

Carmen stayed in contact with Evelyn, and also attended the University of Tennessee before moving on to North Carolina University for her Masters and PhD in Anthropology several years ago. I have my suspicions that Dr. Rainwater might have had something to do with Evelyn's change of heart, and mind, in foregoing her civil engineering training and pursuing a new career path in anthropology.

"My biggest worry is if the reports I found online an hour ago are accurate," Evelyn continued, revisiting the stove for her second cup of cocoa. "Maybe I shouldn't talk about this in front of Chris?"

"I've probably seen or heard worse from the student body at Littleton High," he said, drawing concerned looks from Miriam and David. "Geez, Mom and Dad... don't tell me things were 'Beaver Cleaver' clean when you were in school."

"He might be right, y'all," said Evelyn, lightheartedly, when Miriam took issue with her youngest child's casual attitude to the seriousness of what he and Jillian could soon face. David shrugged when Miriam looked to him for support, and I caught a glimpse of recognition for a similar cavalier attitude when he was teenager. "And, really, the knowledge we gain from here on out might be better served to share it with Jill and Chris. It's only a matter of time before Brigindo ventures beyond Devil Mountain—and God help us if the others join her."

Probably not the thing to share when trying to convince two uneasy adults to allow their cherished cubs to peek at Brigindo's murderous handiwork. Evelyn glanced at me as if suddenly aware of my ever-increasing concern.

"Grandpa, I'm not going to show them the pictures I found that are purportedly from the crime scene yesterday," she advised. "For one thing, they could be fakes, since nothing has been officially released up until now. And, unlike what you're thinking, I don't want to frighten them needlessly.... Just a healthy dose of caution is all I'm intending to instill in them."

Evelyn pulled out her iPad and returned to the dining table where the rest of us were seated. She was already retrieving the information she had gathered earlier, and as promised, she kept the screen out of Chris and Jill's direct line of sight... at least for the moment.

"There's no need to look—especially until these pictures are confirmed as authentic," Evelyn told Jillian, who seemed to have taken greater offense than Chris, since at eighteen years she would be considered an adult in most circles. "What's important is the unconfirmed report of three of the bodies being completely drained of blood... the mother and the two youngest children. The father and the oldest boy were brutally attacked, too... but not drained."

"Meaning what?" asked Chris, creeping closer to where she sat, along with Jillian. "Did the vampire get full?" He laughed nervously.

"The father and son were torn apart," said Evelyn, protectively lifting the iPad from the table and clutching it close to her chest. "You might be closer to the truth of things than you realize, Chris, since if the entities are like Teutates in any way, they would be vampiric in nature. There aren't any photographs of those two victims, and the shots that show the mother and younger children were taken from a distance— likely by a forensic tech that isn't in a hurry to get fired by being caught taking unauthorized photographs from a closer vantage point. And that's if the shots were actually taken from the home above the ravine in Blankenship Pines. They could be from anywhere... opportunists are out there, and this has been national news since Sunday morning."

"But you think Brigindo did this for sure?" David asked, sipping his cocoa.

"Don't you?" she replied. "We just witnessed an unusual looking creature that fits one of the older descriptions I gave Grandpa about a week ago. It—or she, I guess I should say— was covered with blood from her mouth to her legs. Who else could the seven-foot monster be?"

Well, so much for keeping that information from the kids.

"You saw her?" Jillian's expression was a mixture of awe and horror. Unfortunately, there was no chance of putting this genie back in a bottle. Chris' countenance mirrored his big sister's, and the opportunity of returning to bed soon had just been negated.

"I'm sorry Miriam and David... it could've waited, but it's where the conversation was headed," Evelyn told them.

"It should've waited," I said.

"It's okay, Evelyn," Miriam assured her, glancing at David, who nodded he was fine with the unexpected revelation of Brigindo's appearance to their kids. "I don't need convincing that the creature we confronted tonight is her—Brigindo. I just wonder if the shroud had anything to do with why she seemed in a hurry to leave us alone. I thought for sure at least one of us wasn't coming home tonight."

David eyed Miriam in surprise. Apparently, he hoped Brigindo's appearance would be where the information leak stopped. Talking like this was exactly what I had wished to avoid, and it didn't take long to realize sleep was going to come at an escalated premium when the conversation finally ended—especially for our youngsters.

"Shroud? Like the ones they used to wrap people in before they were laid in a tomb?" Chris sounded excited. "We talked about ossuaries and shrouds in social studies this past year in school, during Easter week when Ms. Johnson talked about the rich person's tomb Jesus was buried in after the crucifixion. And, I heard John mention four ossuaries yesterday when he and Dad were talking about coming here."

"Tell us more about Brigindo and the shroud, Mom," said Jillian, pleadingly, avoiding her father's scowl.

"Grandpa, I'm sorry to disappoint you... but if this is a natural place where things are going, then I have to assume Jill and Chris need this information much sooner than later," said Evelyn, her tone emphatic. I understood it wasn't intentional for my granddaughter to divulge the information, and likely the effort to avoid it felt unnatural to her. Sudden warmth touched my shoulder, and I couldn't help but smile, though weakly. *A spirit's touch?* I pictured Two Eagles Cry, my grandfather, smiling as well. He would likely applaud Evelyn for trusting her instincts. Evelyn returned my smile with a stronger one and looked at David, who shook his head worriedly.

"I think Evelyn's right, hon'," Miriam told him, demurely. "There's no way to tell Jill and Chris what's going on without a few frightening details. Not without endangering them by leaving out the reasons why they need to be even more careful than we've been. Who's to say Brigindo won't figure out how to physically materialize away from the ravine? She managed to show up as an apparition in Tennessee last week before the murders…. How much more lucid and deadly would she be now, and in someplace much closer—like here? And if she approached Chris and Jill without them understanding what she is and intends…."

She looked away, and her eyes were misting. But her words seemed to soften David's rigid stance.

We ended up openly discussing everything that had happened earlier that night. Admittedly, I was surprised at the maturity Jillian and Chris demonstrated in handling the information and answers they received to their questions. When we finished tying the night's earlier events to what we had already understood about the ravine and its malevolent occupants, we set our sights on what Carmen Rainwater might be able to do for us.

The hope was for her influence to get the state of North Carolina to permanently stop the construction going on in Blankenship Pines, as well as anywhere else near Devil Mountain. Hindering Brigindo's efforts to free her siblings seemed almost as important as figuring out how to get the demon back inside her ossuary and sealed below the earth's surface once more. And, even though this wasn't a Native American site per se, other than being a place long loathed by the Cherokee Nation, the ancient artifacts should be treated as significant. After all, they pointed to a civilization that visited North America centuries before Columbus landed in the West Indies. For better or worse, they were a significant part of America's heritage.

Finally, we retired as a group around three o'clock Tuesday morning. Evelyn assisted me in making certain her earlier efforts to bless and protect the Hobbs' suite remained in place. As far as we could tell, the family was fully protected from an invasion while they slept. The same thing was soon set up for our suite, as well. Even so, sleep didn't come for me until after four—the last time I remember looking at the alarm clock's digital readout on the nightstand.

A dreamless break for me, we had planned to sleep in until almost noon, with brunch at the local restaurant on the hotel property being our launching point for what we hoped would be a productive afternoon. However, Evelyn and I didn't make it past nine o'clock, as our internal clocks held sway. Perhaps it was for the best, since once we tuned in to the latest televised local news report, the day's plans took on a greater sense of urgency.

"Well, at least things will get interesting now for Simon Blankenship," I grimly advised, after Evelyn and I stood in dumbfounded silence in front of the main television for several minutes. "He will now have to deal with a deeper police probe than he was expecting… could be even worse for business."

In the midst of getting an update on the day's weather forecast, a 'breaking news story' interrupted the details of a series of thunderstorms moving through the area that afternoon and evening. Hopefully, the police had finished their work on finding the rest of Peter Hundley and Joe Swanson's remains before the adverse weather hit. Otherwise it could be a bigger mess.

The report subtly indicated the men's bodies were partially discovered, and in pieces. The police had cordoned off a large area surrounding a walking trail located in the same vicinity as the ravine at Blankenship Pines. The search for 'more clues' was mentioned during the report, and I took it to mean 'more body parts' and perhaps a weapon the authorities would never find.

"I see the faces of the men in my mind's eye… and they are the ones I saw hassling you when you went to visit the development for the first time, Grandpa," Evelyn advised, her voice barely above a whisper.

"I see them, too… and my vision shows the reaction of the early morning jogger who came across an unexpected and unpleasant surprise today," I said. "If my scope of vision is accurate, then Brigindo has far bigger plans than simply releasing her siblings so they can move deeper into the mountains and retreat from mankind."

"What do you mean?"

"Did you not see the severed heads of these two men?"

She nodded slightly, as if acknowledging my question would somehow give more power to the malicious goddess.

"They were impaled on wooden branches stripped of the bark and driven deep into the ground, like the ceremonial stakes used in ancient Gaul… or so my guides told me," she said. "Brigindo isn't planning on going anywhere, which makes her even more dangerous. She will fight to stay in the realm of Devil Mountain. And, I believe she will soon see us as a threat to that plan, if she hasn't already."

I thought about what Galiena said about four new victims, and the absence of the other two from the news report made me wonder when the next discovery would become known to the growing mass of Americans tuning into the story about the rising death toll in North Carolina. No doubt, most would initially look at the carnage as the work of deranged serial killers—which wasn't far from the truth, considering what Galiena had shared about the ancient deities' bloodthirsty habits. However, considering Brigindo's history and the likelihood she was just getting warmed up, the nation—and the world—might soon see a mass murder spree on the scale of a terrorist invasion.

"We can't let that happen, Grandpa," Evelyn advised, alerting me to the fact my mental guard remained compromised enough for her to readily steal images from my thoughts. "The key is making sure the other entities can't physically escape their ossuaries."

"We couldn't get close enough to see them last night—how can we know if they've been broken or not?" It seemed logical that at least one of the other tombs had either been discovered or inadvertently crushed by a backhoe or grader.

"I know you said Galiena can't reach you here... so you're going to have to trust my intuitions—despite what your visions might show as contradictory to them," she said. "I don't think the other three have been damaged yet, but that status could soon change. It depends on what Brigindo is capable of... something tells me she can't free her brothers and sister as easily as I had previously assumed. I hope it's true."

"Me too."

Evelyn was able to get in touch with Carmen Rainwater, who agreed to meet with us at her office near the Cherokee Center at Western Carolina University. As my granddaughter explained to me, Dr. Rainwater had stepped away from her directorship to pursue other interests—namely the anthropological needs of the Cherokee people.

The meeting was set for two o'clock that afternoon, and after brunch with the Hobbs clan, all six of us climbed into the dented Chevy for the thirty-minute drive to Dr. Rainwater's office. David considered taking an immediate insurance hit and switching out the car at the local Avis dealer. However, Evelyn wanted Carmen to see the damage from our encounter with Brigindo, stating it should expedite getting the help we needed to permanently shut down Blankenship Pines.

Carmen was taller than I had expected, perhaps hindered by my remembrance of her as a child the last time I saw her in person. Her striking appearance as a young woman, however, was as I expected from my mind's eye.

"You probably still see me as a little girl, John," she said, as if reading my mind after Evelyn handled the introductions to the Hobbs family. I worried more about the privacy of my thoughts, or apparent lack thereof. "I still remember ice cream on the beach in Wilmington, when you and Susanne took me, Evelyn, and Hanna there."

"We sat on the pier and watched the tide… I remember," I said, smiling at one of the few fond memories I had of that time. Joanna was recovering in the apartment she shared with the girls and the Navy boyfriend I mentioned earlier. I should clarify that Joanna was recovering from a beating, and the sorry S.O.B. was nowhere in sight. Otherwise, I might be keeping a journal of a different kind from behind bars, after making sure the bastard never hurt anybody ever again.

I had often thought Carmen and our girls could pass as sisters, with similar skin tone and the dark eyes and hair of our people. Not to mention dimpled smiles…. I got the feeling she would've been delighted to join us in our dangerous adventure, if not for a busy schedule working on a number of issues involving Native American affairs. Not all dealt with strictly Cherokee concerns, based on what I gathered from the small talk between her and Evelyn.

Carmen brought us into a small boardroom she shared with several other professionals—including two attorneys and a

CPA whose office David took an interest in seeing. It was while she was offering refreshments of coffee, tea, and a soda for Chris that I began to experience a queer feeling. And it came before she broke the latest news to us that a morning cook employed by a roadside restaurant not far from Blankenship Pines was found dead and stuffed inside a trash receptacle behind the restaurant. The discovery was made less than twenty minutes before our arrival, and it was too early to determine if the cook's murder was related to what happened at the construction site.

Not sure if the news was what jolted me from my body. But I soon found myself floating above everyone else and then drifting away toward a lush landscape I had not seen since childhood. Even before I heard Galiena's voice from behind me, I knew this was a shamanistic vision, since the last time I was in this place I was accompanied by my grandfather.

Galiena called to me, and when I turned to face her I was pulled rapidly through miles of forest until I reached a clearing. She approached from a beautiful ravine with a gorgeous waterfall high above us. A swift-moving stream flowed past where I stood, and it took me a moment to recognize this place… the same spot where the entities' bones were now buried.

"They killed the land and the water of life," she told me. "It has been dead for over one thousand years. And now they will spread the same destruction that once plagued my father's people in the land across the ocean. Searix and his men brought them here… to be buried and forgotten forever. You must stop her, Running Deer!"

"But how?" I asked. "How can I do it without your help? Or, has something changed to where you can finally assist me?"

"Abellio is no longer waiting for me, and I fear he will soon join her in the land of the living...."

She was distraught—I discerned it from her energy, which made her trembling form transparent. Her deep blue eyes were seas of profound sadness. She felt personally responsible for Brigindo's escape—even though it was men like Simon Blankenship that made the decision to keep digging in the ravine after Brigindo's ossuary had been discovered.

"It *is* my fault... I should have reached out to you sooner, Running Deer," she continued. "Brigindo is gaining strength from the blood of her victims, as you and Evelyn have correctly assessed. She is almost strong enough to release the others, but is seeking something else... something about the mix of blood. Something...." She shook her head, unable to pinpoint what the murderous goddess was after.

"We are trying to stop the construction—can we not reverse it?" I asked, hoping for something positive to cling to.

"Only if her bones are returned to her tomb," she said. "You must retrieve and rebury them before she finds what she is looking for and breaks through the spell binding the others."

"How in the hell am I supposed to make that happen— especially when I have no clue where her bones are at the moment?" I protested, finding it hard to not get angry. "I mean, do you know where they are? Is it like Teutates, when he kept his bones near his bloody altar?"

"I don't know where she has hidden her bones. But there is still time to find them," she said. "But you can't wait on the scholars your granddaughter is hoping her friend can put her in contact with. That could take weeks, and you only have a matter of days before it is finally too late."

"What can we do, then?" I felt defeated, although willing to try almost anything.

"Think about it, Running Deer—and find the answer to *this* question*,* " she said, turning as if ready to leave. I suddenly couldn't move, and realized in surprise she wasn't moving away from me—I was being drawn away from her. "Six years ago, when Hanna was assumed in trouble, as well as Evelyn, Miriam, and David…. What did you do?"

I awoke with a start, surprised to find everyone gathered around my chair at the table. Evelyn appeared to be crying, probably worried sick since I had never fallen into a trance like this one in her presence. And if the vision came with convulsing, she might've ignored her true discernment and likely thought I was having a stroke or heart attack.

The only good thing was that once the trance ended, I knew immediately what to do. But it wasn't something I wanted to announce or fulfill.

We needed to return to the ravine as soon as possible.

Chapter Ten

Other than Evelyn, I didn't expect anyone present to understand what happened in the boardroom. A full explanation seemed unwarranted due to Dr. Rainwater's presence. Even though she worked tirelessly on behalf of the Cherokee Nation, in no way did that mean she was a believer in the old 'mystical' ways from centuries past. Evelyn had told me long ago that Carmen supported my granddaughter's use of her extrasensory gifts. Yet, despite Carmen's strong intuitions and apparent open mind, until I knew for certain she embraced the shaman traditions of our people, sharing my vision could do more harm than good if it turned out that she didn't. As for the Hobbs foursome, I knew I'd have to offer some kind of explanation to keep from visiting the local hospital, since David had suffered a heart attack scare two years ago and likely saw mirrored symptoms in me that were similar enough to what he experienced back then.

"Should I tell them, or should you?" I asked Evelyn, once she realized from my description of the ravine's pristine appearance that I had been overcome by a vision. She had witnessed such events when she visited the Sioux Nation out west some years ago, and they allowed her to witness their shamanistic practices. At the time, there were only a handful of 'active' Native American shamans from across America. It wasn't until after her visit to South Dakota that she learned I had resisted the calling.

"My grandfather just now received a vision facilitated by his guide, Galiena," she told Carmen, who nodded thoughtfully in response.

I should add here that part of my concern about Dr. Rainwater was her ability to cloak her thoughts—something I had noticed about her when she was a little girl. The trait was more developed now that she was older—likely fed by heartache, as Evelyn once mentioned she took the passing of her grandmother and mother very hard.

"What did your guide tell you, John?" Carmen asked.

"The forces murdering innocent people are ancient, and have resided undisturbed at the foot of Devil Mountain for many centuries," I told her. "That is, until Simon Blankenship desecrated their resting place in a ravine within the development called Blankenship Pines."

"I know of this place. It's been on the news for the past week. It's also the one Evelyn mentioned on the phone, and we've received a number of complaints from the reservation about it," she said. "Now, eight people have been killed and maybe more. So, go on... please."

Dr. Rainwater had assumedly agreed with Evelyn that the cook stuffed into a dumpster was a victim of Brigindo's murderous rage. I previously thought Evelyn hadn't shared Galiena's assertion about one other victim yet to be discovered. That would make nine deaths with many more likely to come. I confirmed the names of the deities buried in the ravine, and then shared the story of how they were transported and buried by Europeans seeking relief from the same malady of death. Carmen also had questions about Galiena, since the name sounded foreign. I advised that it was a name popular in ancient Germania, and Evelyn added what she recently learned about 'Galiena' still being used as a name in rural Italy.

"We need to go back there today," I said, once I explained to everyone the details of the ravine's former beauty, and how the four entities' presence had drained the very life out of the area. They would soon do the same on a much grander scale if we didn't find and rebury the remains of Brigindo, and secure the other three ossuaries below the earth's surface. "In fact, we need to go there *right now.*"

"Grandpa, the place is likely crawling with police—including the federal authorities," Evelyn advised. "It won't be anything like last night, when the entire development was deserted."

Of course, Evelyn was right. I wished I could go to the site alone and take my chances. If I were arrested, or worse, it would just be me who would suffer the consequences. Perhaps Galiena could accompany me this time, although my heart told me that her influence would again disappear the moment the beautiful blue mountain came into view from the highway.

But I wouldn't be alone, necessarily. Galiena had given me the answer I needed, and to be honest, I silently berated myself for not seeing it earlier. It was simple, and once she presented the scenario involving Hanna—and later included Evelyn, Miriam, and David—the answer to 'what did I do?' was clear.

I had called on *Tali Awohali Atloyasdi* back then, the Cherokee name of my grandfather, Two Eagles Cry.

At that time he took on the appearance of a wolf, leading me through the darkened halls of Teutates' temple beneath the "lovers' lane" ravine in Cades Cove. Without his help, I would have arrived too late to rescue my family and friends from a horrifying end…. Could his spirit come through for me once again?

Galiena believed so, and having served as his guide more than sixty years earlier, she would be in position to make such a recommendation.

"I realize it won't be the same as it was last night," I said, "But what's to stop us from taking a look at things from the road, Evelyn? We might pick up on something… and maybe this time Galiena will be there to help us determine the status of the other tombs."

She nodded as if considering the idea might actually have merit, as did David. Miriam looked on blankly. I believed she and the kids were going to follow whatever direction we decided upon. Carmen appeared unconvinced this was a good idea, and understandably so.

"Brigindo's ossuary was unearthed and damaged by Blankenship's men, and Grandpa saw the bones protruding from the side of the box last week. But when we viewed the box yesterday, the bones were gone," Evelyn explained to her. "We did consider the possibility they were stolen by someone. Now that the guards hassling Grandpa are dead, it's likely Brigindo retrieved the bones herself."

"And, by yesterday, you do mean last night." Dr. Rainwater eyed Evelyn and me seriously. "Correct?"

"Yes," said Evelyn. "I guess we were trespassing… but so is anyone who dares to invade the grounds of *Tsvsgina Odalv.*"

"Yes, I would agree. I'm quite familiar with the legends of Devil Mountain that have been part of Cherokee folklore since well before the English set foot in Appalachia," said Carmen. A slight smile tugged on the corners of her lips. "I suppose it wouldn't be trespassing to drive by there, although I doubt we'll get much further than the main entrance to Blankenship Pines."

"That's all we should need to make a determination," I said. "If either Two Eagles Cry or Galiena are unsuccessful in telling me how to safely determine the ossuaries' status, we'll move on."

"Grandpa, you're not planning to trespass or interfere with the police investigation, are you?" Evelyn asked, gazing at me the way Carmen had regarded us a moment ago.

Only if the opportunity presents itself and either Galiena or Grandfather tells me "Go for it!"

"I only want to have a casual look around—no interference planned," I assured her.

Admittedly, a survey of the ravine held during daylight hours would be the more attractive choice—regardless of a multiple homicide investigation going on. Yet, the notion of it being safer was unsupportable—even with the silly hope of Brigindo and her kin possibly being hindered by the sun's ultraviolet rays, like the vampire legends of old. The idea was most appealing, until I recalled Galiena's earlier *Akasha* visions, and Searix and his European pals running for their lives through the forest to reach the Atlantic coast with the four angry deities hot on their tails. The sun shined brightly that day, and the ill-tempered gods and goddesses were unaffected by it as they slaughtered men and drank their blood.

"Evelyn… how about you and John ride with me?" Carmen suggested. "That way I can make sure everyone remains upstanding citizens during our visit. We'll get as close as possible to the site you seek, and go from there."

"That sounds like the best plan," said Evelyn, after David and Miriam confirmed that they'd follow Carmen's vehicle in the Chevy.

Facing the likelihood that I'd be confined inside Dr. Rainwater's car, I resigned myself to making the best of the situation. I held out hope that maybe the forensic teams scouring the area for additional clues would be finished by the time we arrived, or miraculously take their lunch break after four o'clock in the afternoon… or perhaps get called away to search somewhere else in the area.

Hope against hope, I was already working on an alternative plan should everything else fall through. Unfortunately, it meant trying one more nighttime visit. But even that would have to wait until an appropriate opportunity presented itself....

"What in the hell?" Carmen's mouth dropped open in awe once she saw the dents in the Chevrolet's roof. In the clear light of day, toe and heel marks from a large naked foot within the dent added immediate credibility to Evelyn's recounting of what had happened the night before, and the angry goddess Brigindo making the depth of her displeasure known to us. "That's some crazy shit, Eve!"

"That's why it's critical to stop construction in the ravine from progressing any further," Evelyn replied. Carmen picked up her pace to reach the Lexus parked not far from the Chevy. Evelyn and I did the same. "We need for it all to cease until we can ensure that the other three tombs remain sealed and we can somehow retrieve what was taken from the tomb belonging to Brigindo."

"You made your point by showing me the dents," said Carmen, motioning for us to climb into her car. "We're going to discuss this in more depth on our way there."

And we did talk about it... or, rather, *they* talked and I listened. All the while I wondered if Evelyn and Carmen would actually try to stop me from visiting the ravine if the opportunity to get a closer look presented itself and I bolted from the car. I confess that I also wondered if Brigindo would try to interfere somehow with my fact-finding mission, since ultimately it could lead to her undoing.

In the end, such speculation proved worthless.

I should've known things would prove unfavorable, based on the traffic to reach Blankenship Pines alone. The exit from the highway was backed-up with cars still on the interstate.

"This is like a frigging rock concert," Evelyn observed. "It looks like it might take a damned hour to get in there! Sorry about this."

"It's okay," Carmen assured her, and then glanced back at me through the rearview mirror. "I kind of expected some traffic, although not nearly as bad as this. Eight murders in the same spot, in a matter of a few days, and taking place at the foot of a mountain described as cursed in local folklore can create that sort of rubbernecking frenzy, I guess. But I would think that most rational people would avoid such a place like the plague.... John, how are you holding up back there?"

"I'm fine." I hoped I sounded calm, but inside I was fuming.

How could we possibly enter the site inconspicuously when a caravan of cars carrying curious Carolinians crept by the brutal crime scene? Even if the police had finished, or had moved on to another area of the site, two vehicles driving through the gates would surely draw a number of other cars from the endless stream of traffic behind us. There would be no way to get a closer look without sticking out like a sore thumb.

I looked back at David driving behind us... he motioned to the line of cars ahead of us and shook his head. Maybe we should've called the whole thing off. But I felt compelled to try and at least pick up something from the ravine. We needed to reach the gated entrance in order for that to be a slim possibility.... Perhaps some kind of message, or mini vision from Galiena, or Two Eagles Cry, would come to me as we slowly drove past the entrance.

It took almost forty minutes to reach the gates.

"What in the hell? ...Look, Grandpa—they've cordoned off the entire entrance!" Evelyn pointed to where all access beyond the main entrance was blocked. Several police vehicles were strategically parked inside and outside the gates, to ensure no unauthorized persons would make it inside Blankenship Pines.

"I'll see what I can pick up from here," I said, figuring it would take us about fifteen minutes to move beyond the area. Plenty of time, in most cases, to pick up something useful or determine if a location was psychically dead.

But we already knew the grounds were alive and quite active. I could feel it from the moment we took the exit, and felt certain that it was the same for Evelyn and likely Carmen, too. The unseen hostility emanating toward the Lexus from deep within this desecrated place had gained strength since the other night.

I closed my eyes to try and determine if Abnoba and her brothers, Abellio and Smetrios were part of the negative energy feeding the wave of malice infiltrating the car. If I could pick out the personality imprints, perhaps I could make an accurate guess as to how many of Brigindo's siblings had escaped their tombs.

Suddenly, as if in response to my disdain for this Gallic brood, the malevolent feeling intensified.

"Do you feel how it's getting worse, Grandpa?"

"Yes… Carmen feels it, too, don't you?"

"I think coming here wasn't such a great idea," said Dr. Rainwater. "This place really gives me the creeps."

Then we heard it… a voice that startled us all. Soft in a female sense, and guttural—as if the language it spoke was new to the owner of the voice. But the words weren't from the English language, and it took us a moment to fully recognize our native tongue being bastardized by a heavy accent.

If only it had been Galiena, and not someone else.

"Anagisdi owenvsv…." *Go home.*

"So… does this mean we're not welcome?" I asked, to no one in particular.

A sardonic chuckle in female timber resounded throughout the car in response, sending shivers down my spine. I assumed it was the same for Evelyn and Carmen, since both whimpered, looking around the front seat nervously.

"Gotivhisodi… nihi nasginigesvna ulihelisdi!" *Correct... you're not welcome!*

"Great we're stuck in traffic with a damned spirit that doesn't want us around!" Carmen's attempt to sound brave couldn't disguise her terror. I picked up a mental picture from her, of the Lexus suddenly transformed into a helicopter and then whisking the three of us to safety.

Another mean chuckle erupted, and I felt the spirit's contempt in response to Carmen's comment, as if to say, "What good would your flight through the air do if I came along for the ride?"

Unwise to engage a malicious spirit when trespassing on its turf, I stifled a disdainful response bridled on the tip of my tongue. It only took a moment for the entity to react.

"Anagisdi owenvsv, Adatlisvi Awiinageehi!" *Go home, Running Deer!*

My blood simmered from the spirit's brashness, using our native tongue in an insolent manner. Unfortunately, the onset of anger tends to make me laugh. Not intending to be rude, it's an instinctive thing. When I laughed this time, Evelyn and Carmen looked back at me in horror—as if I brazenly intended to further agitate our unwelcome visitor.

"Anagisdi owenvsv, Adatlisvi Awiinageehi…. *NAQUU!"* *Go home, Running Deer…. NOW!*

The seething inhuman shout was enough to wipe the smirk from my face. But our visitor wasn't finished making a point. A powerful gust slammed into the car from outside, almost tipping it over. In the midst of terrified screaming going on in the front seat, I watched as David and Miriam left their vehicle and tried to open the Lexus' doors that remained locked despite Carmen and Evelyn pounding on the door switches. Our would-be rescuers might not have heard the initial threats from the unseen menace, but the sudden frightened looks on their faces revealed they definitely heard the latest roar of displeasure.

"Anagisdi owenvsv, Adatlisvi Awiinageehi! Nihi nasginigesvna ulihelisdi ahani… *IYUQUU!*" *Go home, Running Deer! You're not welcome here… EVER!*

Chapter Eleven

"We must leave and never come back here."

Words spoken from my heart, I had adopted our antagonist's point of view. We weren't welcome, would never be welcome, and the longer we stayed the more dangerous things would become.

"I am sorry to have dragged you all into this," I continued. "Please forgive me... everyone."

"Grandpa, what happened back there scared the holy shit out of me—out of Carmen, too," said Evelyn. "But I don't know that leaving here with our tails between our legs is the right thing to do…. Is this what Galiena wants? And your grandfather—my ancestor, too—what would Two Eagles Cry think of our courage, or the lack of it?"

We were gathered once again in the common area of Evelyn's and my suite at the Fairview Inn. The remnants of our dinner sat in the mostly empty boxes from a local popular pizzeria. Meanwhile, the latest TV news report included news of another homicide discovery. This one involved a family living less than a mile from Blankenship Pines in a double-wide trailer. All four people—two adults and two children—were dead. Although the details were sketchy, Evelyn and I had picked up the same thing... eventual details regarding this terrible crime would mimic what befell the family slaughtered in the massive home overlooking the ravine.

The official death toll was at twelve, although certainly this latest news didn't include the other undisclosed killing mentioned by Galiena. *Thirteen and counting*.... Could be even more by now.

"How can I know what Galiena wants when she is pushed away the very moment we get near the place?" I quietly lamented. "Two Eagles Cry wouldn't be happy with a retreat—true, especially now that the death toll is climbing. And if it was only my well being to worry about, I would return to the ravine alone.... But I already know that you'd insist on coming, Evelyn."

"As would I," said David.

"Me, too," added Miriam.

The kids stated their commitment as well, and it was quickly shot down by David and echoed by Miriam. The cubs would have to stay put, regardless of who signed up to join me in what appeared to be an inevitable nighttime trip into Hell on Earth. My mindset at the moment was to find some other way around a confrontation my heart assured me that we'd lose, and lose badly. Flight seemed like the best immediate option—and in my mind, it was no different than when my ancestors who retreated deep into the Smokies did so to avoid the forced march along the Trail of Tears. Conceding ground in order to regroup and reassess a problem for a better solution was in no way cowardice. Even if it meant never returning to Devil Mountain.

"Damned straight, I'm coming with you," said Evelyn. She gazed at me curiously, surely catching the jumble of unpleasant images in my head. "But I wish you'd settle down and quit talking about us leaving before Carmen can get back to me. She told me to be patient with Dr. Hewitt. He'll get back to us sometime in the next few days—by Friday at the latest. If we give up and leave, my heart tells me that we'll just have to come back again at some point. I guarantee whatever we encountered today will be a hundred times worse by then....

Besides, Grandpa, what will you do if Brigindo or any of the others follow us back to Tennessee?"

I had worried about that very thing before we decided to come to North Carolina as a group, since Brigindo had already pursued us to Tennessee in spirit. In truth, there wasn't a right or wrong answer as to what we should do. Waiting in Cherokee for an answer from a college professor, who may or may not be able to help us, or returning home to Tennessee carried enormous risks.

As for Dr. Hewitt, he was a close colleague and friend of Dr. Rainwater. Currently, he headed the American Indian and Indigenous Studies department at the University of North Carolina. Carmen—and Evelyn—believed he gave us the best chance to get the ravine protected from further development. Perhaps he could also help prevent exploitation of the ancient ossuaries and their contents. Perhaps... but no guarantees.

"Maybe Miriam, you, and the kids should go back to Colorado, as I've suggested before," I told David. "I know it's not what you want to hear... but if it means staying out of harm's way, we can always get together in the fall out there. Weren't we going to visit Garden of the Gods the last time we came? I recall how the weather was beautiful, and it can be even better in September—"

"Fat chance of us leaving you and Evelyn to the wolves!" David interrupted me. "I could never live with myself if something happened to you or to Evelyn, and we weren't here to protect you both from getting in over your heads."

I nodded thoughtfully, though my opinion remained the same. A glance at Evelyn revealed a look that told me her thoughts were similar to mine.

"How would you two feel about coming home with us to Colorado right now?" Miriam asked. "I mean, after you wait to see if you hear back from Dr. Hewitt. If it turns out he can't be of immediate help, rather than wait for disaster to strike here or back at John's cabin, maybe it would be best to leave this region of the country—at least for now."

I started to decline her offer, but Evelyn stopped me. I believe that Miriam's offer would've been an easy one for her to sidestep a week ago… but after the events of the past two days it made sense. I was forced to consider that if Dr. Hewitt's potential help failed to materialize, could we rationally refuse a lifesaver thrown to us in shark-infested waters?

"Thank you, Miriam, for your gracious proposal," I said. "How about it, Evelyn? Would you consider the offer if Dr. Hewitt either fails to respond or provides an inadequate solution?"

Despite my granddaughter's intrigue, which was obvious to me, she didn't give an answer right away. She had originally resisted the idea of coming to North Carolina to remedy the situation, yet now seemed to struggle with admitting defeat and agreeing to pull the plug on our efforts to restore peace to the ravine and surrounding areas. If we left without a resolution in place, could we live with ourselves if the demons' newfound freedom brought much worse carnage to the region?

Images of rampant bloodshed afflicting areas far beyond the shadow of Devil Mountain suddenly appeared in my mind. Perhaps this was based on irrational fears only, but how could I know for certain?

"I agree… it's an attractive offer, Grandpa," said Evelyn, regarding me solemnly. "I can take care of my studies online from out of state, as you know, if we stayed away from Tennessee for a while. But your fears about the other potential consequences are far from irrational and must also be considered."

I was too tired emotionally to challenge her for disclosing my thoughts verbatim. I nodded a weak acknowledgement.

"In the very least, it will be as bad as you pictured," she continued. "The world will mourn a massacre they could scarcely understand. And worse? There may be other fiends buried in this region and elsewhere that are just as vile, restless, and hungry. Once these four are loose, who's to say they won't find the others and set them free?"

Including Teutates?

"Okay… this is the part where the two of you need to stop keeping secrets from the rest of us—at least from Miriam and me—about what you see coming," said David. "I believe my wife and I deserve to know exactly what's headed our way." He glanced at Miriam who heartily agreed.

I had felt their shared frustration from across the room earlier while I considered Evelyn's response to my silent musings. Their beef was valid… but I first needed to clarify the additional mental images Evelyn picked up on a moment ago. I hadn't considered the likelihood of other demons buried in the Smoky Mountains region, though it made sense when I remembered the terrifying haunting behind the Bell Witch legend of middle Tennessee. The powerful entity behind that haunting was able to imitate the voices of local residents and drop fruit from the West Indies into Lucy Bell's lap. The spirit later murdered her husband, John Bell.

Andrew Jackson, whose unwarranted persecution of my ancestors has been well documented, stated long ago that he was more frightened of this particular entity than the entire British army. Not your typical ghost by any stretch, it certainly supported the idea of other discarded deities from prior cultures lying in wait for rediscovery beneath the earth's surface.

"It might not be possible to make such a commitment, David—since many of the images that have come to either of us lately have arrived without warning. I assure you that it's not our intent to leave either of you in the dark," I advised.

"Perhaps we can make a better effort to let you know sooner.... I can tell that you both have questions about the earlier 'reign of terror' from these entities that was visited upon ancient Gaul and later Germania and its bordering nations. Correct?"

They nodded somberly. At least their curiosity wasn't anything like the wide-eyed fascination of Chris and Jillian.

"I don't think we need to discuss things in the graphic detail revealed by Searix's memories," said Evelyn, obviously concerned about the effect it might have on the kids. Despite dealing directly with the angry wraith of Allie Mae McCormick, both Jillian and Chris were spared a confrontation with Teutates. No doubt, experiencing what David and Miriam had witnessed back then would've more than satisfied the younger Hobbs' curiosity, and likely forever.

"Holding back the brutality only lessens the impact of how dangerous the entities are," said David. "Sorry to say, but yours and John's description of Brigindo paled horribly to the real monster altering our rental car's appearance."

"Did you ever tell Tyler, Jill, and Chris about what the four of us saw lined up in front of Teutates' bloody altar?" I asked, hating to revisit the vileness of the temple beneath Cades Cove—a place that had delivered numerous nightmares to Evelyn and me.

David looked over at Miriam again, who this time provided little support, shaking her head as if reliving the horror of being forced to witness the atrocities delivered by the demon that day.

"I'm sorry Miriam and David... what Searix observed more than a thousand years ago isn't any different than what the two of you witnessed, along with us," I said, hoping my tone matched the compassion in my heart. "If you haven't felt comfortable enough to talk about it with Jill and Chris, then sharing the slaughter of hundreds of innocent people over the course of a few decades in Searix's life—before he and his fellow sailors set their sights on dumping the vile deities' bones in the New World—would be even more disturbing, I fear. And it was even worse when these angered gods and goddesses tore open the bodies of Searix's comrades who had set out to bury the five ossuaries in our country."

"I would like to hear about it, if you don't mind, John," said Jillian, echoed enthusiastically by Chris. "Mom and Dad have told us a few general things about what happened to them... like stuff about people's heads lying around Teutates' altar." She sounded a bit too excited, and Evelyn and I exchanged worried looks.

"We hated telling the kids that much," admitted Miriam. "It was important to try to protect them, so we kept the unpleasant details to a minimum. We never dreamed we'd be facing the same shit again.... Are you sure Brigindo and the others are as bad as *he* was?"

"Worse," said Evelyn. "Teutates is a terrible menace by himself. But the potential of his four siblings on the loose would bring a level of horror this country has never known, except when at war, where the casualties are equally gruesome and the death toll high."

"Don't forget these creatures are cunning, and can kill in ways that doesn't draw attention to them," I said. "They're like clever serial killers who glean victims from populous areas and move on before anything is detected out of place.... They could hunt like this for decades before revealing themselves to the populace at large.... Or they could bypass the charade and attack unsuspecting communities in a sudden rage."

Images seared forever in my mind from what I had witnessed through Searix's eyes came to life again—rejuvenated by me talking about the centuries' reign of terror wielded by the demons over terrified kingdoms. Granted, the folks living back then lacked any of the weaponry and technology we have at our disposal today.... But what would it take to destroy these creatures using a current arsenal? When swords, arrows, and catapults loaded with burning boulders failed to leave a lasting scratch, would bullets and bombs fare any better?

The only thing that had saved the ancient peoples of Europe was the magic used to confine all five entities to ossuaries that seemed foolproof unless destroyed or desecrated. And even then, the tombs were only effective in limiting the amount and scope of attacks. It led back to our original quandary of how to sneak inside Blankenship Pines and invade the ravine to locate and secure the ossuaries without getting arrested, or torn apart by Brigindo and any of the other deities that might've recently escaped their imprisonment.

Nothing was resolved that night, other than to resume the discussion in the morning with the resolution to finalize contingency plans by Wednesday evening. That would leave us two more days at most to wait on Dr. Hewitt. By Friday night, we were either going to act on his advice—as long as it was something practical—or head home to collect Shawn from my buddy Butch Silva, who recently retired from the Sevierville Sheriff's Department.

Lying in bed thinking about everything that had happened the past two days, I finally began to drift off to sleep shortly after eleven. Just before crossing over into the world of dreams, I became aware of a familiar presence—one that had been weakened since my first visit to Cherokee.

Galiena?

She was somewhere close by, or at least she felt physically closer than she had since I first left Tennessee the week before. I felt something lightly touch my foot and was jolted awake.

A solid figure stood at the foot of my bed in shadow. But I was not alarmed… a feeling of love emanated toward me. As it did, the essence of this person began to glow subtly—enough to where I could detect the features of Galiena's favored appearance in the bedroom's dimness. Only it was different than before—as though she were actually standing before me in the flesh! I could smell the buckskin scent of her clothes, along with her hair fresh from a waterfall's cleansing followed by the sun's rays to dry.

I started to sit up and welcome her to my room, but she motioned for me to remain in my bed. When I started to speak, she shushed me.

"Don't speak… listen," she whispered, her voice less musical than before. "Listen and respond with your thoughts, Running Deer."

I was amazed by the earthiness of her presence, and silently questioned if this was some kind of mind trick that had hijacked a dream.

"No… I am real," she assured me. "The ethereal world is charged by Brigindo's influence, and it has allowed me to materialize more fully than I have ever been able to do since leaving the realm of the living. But that is not why I am here…. I listened to your conversation with Evelyn and David this evening, and I am compelled to warn you about what lies ahead. I am very sorry that I ever dragged you into this…."

Of course, I felt alarmed by her words, and knew beyond all doubt that what my heart had told me earlier was most certainly the truth. The entities continued to move closer to freedom, and Brigindo had found a way to make it happen.

"Not yet, but yes… she has weakened the restraint of the ravine's hold on them all, although just slightly," she said. "I can now clearly see why Brigindo is frustrated. All four must travel together…. Before he died, Adalbern laid a boundary for them. Intended to keep the four deities together in the ravine, the barrier failed in that regard, as you know. However, it has prevented Brigindo from venturing beyond the realm of Devil Mountain for long without her siblings. They are bound together at present, and she is furious. Furthermore, Adalbern also put seals in place for each tomb. Except for hers, all have held up. She can't manifest the destruction of the other ossuaries, like what happened to hers when the modern man tools destroyed it. The blood she has taken from the innocent and poured onto the ground above each tomb has only awakened her brothers and sisters, but it can't set them free. They remain in bondage, where their anger seethes unabated. If, or more likely *when,* they do escape, may the Great Spirit show mercy to the innocent citizens in this region unaware of what's coming."

Her emphasis on 'when' sent a chill down my spine.

"But remember what I said about the blood? Brigindo senses that either you or Evelyn carries what she needs for complete freedom and restoration of a world she and the others once ruled without mercy. And, yet, she warned you not to return to the ravine…. I am confused as to why, but know she is up to something. I believe she may have found a way to release at least one of her siblings in order to help her get what she needs from you…."

I felt confused, too, and started to speak when she shushed me again.

"The one you need to worry about most, Running Deer, is Smetrios," she continued. "He is the worst of them all, almost as wicked as Teutates. I can feel his rage and hear his threats from beneath the ground…. If loosed upon the Earth, he will slaughter without mercy, seeking the meekest ones since they won't resist being bludgeoned by his club or seared by the firebrand he carries. Unholy serpents crawl upon his shoulders and will seek out new victims. It will be nothing for this one to slay a thousand in a single night."

Can he harm us now? I wondered, picturing Smetrios rising from the earth and traveling to the Fairview Inn, perhaps disposing of a few dozen gamblers across the street at the casino on his merry way to visit our rented suites.

"No... not yet. But for how much longer will you and your loved ones remain safe? It depends on whether you stay or leave." A wave of sadness washed over me, and Galiena hung her head for a moment. I detected sniffles and again was affected by how real she seemed, the experience incredibly profound. "I can't force you to stay, Running Deer, and what I tell you next may influence your urge to flee this place forever."

"What do you mean?" I asked, again forgetting to be verbally silent and let my mind do the talking. She motioned for me to be still.

"Here is what I gathered from Smetrios conversations with Brigindo, telling her what they need in order to break the bonds," said Galiena. "Adalbern sealed the tombs with his own blood, perhaps believing his status as a druid descendant would protect him and his comrades from harm. And, since Brigindo now knows yours and Evelyn's status as shamans, she wants whichever of you is strongest to be the vessel she uses to break the seals, free her siblings, and release all other bonds that have imprisoned her family to some extent or another for the past twenty-five hundred years."

"But I'm not even a practicing shaman—neither is Evelyn," I protested, this time silently.

"It matters not... it runs in your veins. Yours and Evelyn's blood is holy due to your exalted status, and Brigindo caught a whiff of it the other night, and again this past afternoon," said

Galiena. "She will sense it again immediately if either of you return to her realm... which is why I am so sorry."

"Don't be... we will make arrangements to head back to Tennessee and then move on to Colorado in the morning," I said. My lingering debate with Evelyn and the Hobbs clan had just been squashed by Galiena's revelation. "I thank you for saving our lives." I meant it, and began thinking of other campaigning we could do to close the site from Colorado, or someplace else if that wasn't far enough away.

"Don't thank me yet," she replied. "I have spoken to Two Eagles Cry, who is also near at this moment.... We agree that for the greater good you should both stay and see to it that the tombs are all reburied."

What in the hell? Didn't she just tell me that Evelyn and I would look like a smorgasbord to these unholy fiends?

"I am willing to risk myself for Evelyn and everyone else," I told her. "But I will send her away *and* keep her away. I will die willingly to spare her life."

"The intent is not to sacrifice anyone's lives... it is merely to present how dangerous your quest will be to return to the ravine," she said. "Sacrificing yourself or Evelyn without a fight will save no one. But it will take you both to get close enough to Brigindo to discover where she has hidden her bones. They need to be placed inside the shroud and reburied in the same spot. The ossuary has been destroyed and can no longer be restored. But with the right blessing upon the shroud and bones, the items can be safely reburied without consequence, despite the cloth of the shroud eventually disintegrating into the earth. Evelyn did this once already for Teutates, and if Brigindo is stopped and her bones reburied, she will remain trapped beneath the earth's surface forever— and it will be the same for the others."

"But we still have to figure out where Brigindo is hiding her bones, right?" I was unable to remove the mental image of my granddaughter and me packing up our prized husky and heading west. "How are we supposed to accomplish that?

Suddenly the uncomfortable charge from earlier Tuesday returned, and as it did, Galiena looked away anxiously. When she returned her gaze to me, her expression was panicked and she mouthed something about 'holding on'.

Hold on to what?

As had recently become her custom, she suddenly vanished.

I wasn't sure what she meant. Thinking about a growing number of possible meanings kept me up until the earliest light of dawn peered in through the bedroom window's curtains. In the end, I couldn't definitively decipher what Galiena desperately sought to tell me. All I knew for sure was that we had to find Brigindo's bones before the demon figured out how to stop us… permanently.

Chapter Twelve

Evelyn was brewing a fresh pot of coffee when I emerged from my room. Showered and ready for the day, we were twin souls in restlessness. She couldn't sleep any better than I did, and now we were faced with filling the next few hours in some meaningful way before Miriam and Jillian would awaken ahead of David and Chris.

"I would ask if you slept at all, but I can see the answer in your eyes," I said, after joining her at the breakfast nook.

"Gee thanks, Grandpa. I look like death warmed over, huh?"

She laughed, but the worry in her eyes had fueled a wakeful night. I wondered if she had somehow heard Galiena's message of doom…. A sudden, deeper cloud that swept across the weariness told me she hadn't.

"What did Galiena tell you?" she asked, worriedly.

"Well, let me first state that I'm getting damned tired of her coming to tell me things and warn me about danger, and then cannot finish her words." I offered a weak smile that did little to dim Evelyn's apprehension. "Why does she do this?"

"If I could see her and converse with her, I would ask that very same question," said Evelyn. "Since a whole lot of good this *isn't* doing us."

"She said to hold on to something, but I have no idea what I'm supposed to hold and whether she meant that literally or not…. She told me the other three deities are now fully awake."

"We already knew that, remember? But it officially explains the negative vibe we felt last night," she advised. "I'm still feeling it, actually."

"Yes... I feel it, too."

"Unless she comes back and tells you what it is you're supposed to hold on to, Grandpa, we're going to have to go with what feels right. It might mean ignoring what she couldn't clarify."

I wondered about the other admonitions Galiena gave me that she seemed to feel the strongest about—about our shaman blood and what she and my grandfather wanted Evelyn and me to do.... *We agree that for the greater good you should stay and see to it that the tombs are all reburied.*

"It's hard to wrap my mind around the thought of Brigindo and Smetrios needing our blood, as if it really is different from anyone else's." Evelyn returned to the kitchen to pour another cup of coffee. "Are you ready for a refill?"

"Not yet... I think what Galiena told me about our bloodline is correct. The veracity of it rings true within my heart of hearts."

"That statement alone makes me want to leave and never come back to this place!" she replied, letting a small plate land noisily in the sink. "Sorry."

"Don't worry about it.... Maybe we should make the effort tonight to try and go to the ravine one last time. Just you and me, without the others."

Really, I wanted to go alone. However, insisting on doing so would likely backfire. Evelyn would not only defy my advice for her to remain at the hotel, but I wouldn't be able to keep David and Miriam from coming along either. It still might not work to restrict tonight's search party to just Evelyn and myself, though it would be especially dangerous for anyone else to come along since I couldn't protect them. Knowing the entities were attracted to Evelyn's blood, and mine, my focus would mostly be on guarding my granddaughter—which could mean sacrificing my life and ignoring any immediate danger to David and Miriam.

"I think it would be best," she agreed, and I felt a layer of her anxiousness begin to dissipate. "But you know David is going to do his damnedest to come along. Miriam seems more prepared to stay with the kids this time, although I know she'd lay her life down for them and him if she was faced with having to make that choice."

"Maybe David will see the wisdom in staying here to protect them all." I absently stirred the remnants of the day's first cup of coffee. "I wish they would go home. Not because I'm ready for them to leave, but I fear something tragic is looming in their future… an event I can't prevent or save them from. Neither can you."

"I thought it was just me thinking that way," said Evelyn, releasing a low sigh. "The timing of their visit seemed so perfect when we finalized the plans in April… and yet now it appears to be a disastrous decision. I wish they would allow us to come see them in just a few months, and return to Colorado immediately."

"So, will you help me work on them… to get them to go home today?" I raised my cup in mock salute.

"Sure… I'll follow your lead." She stood up suddenly and retreated to her room. "I have something to show you."

She soon returned with her laptop and brought it over to the nook.

"Carmen shared some excerpts from old local diaries that she emailed to me last night," said Evelyn, turning the laptop's screen so we could both view it. "Since I couldn't sleep worth a damn, I got an early start on reading these a few hours ago…. The one that's most interesting is from a local clergyman in

Asheville who befriended the Cherokee nation. His name was Jeremiah Cotter, and here's a passage from his diary where he mentioned a blue mountain—'spectacular in beauty', but where even the fiercest warriors refused to go anywhere near."

The excerpt was dated May 15th, 1688, and spanned several pages. Reverend Cotter detailed the hardships of having to travel for several additional weeks to reach an English settlement located not far from where the Cherokee reservation sits today. From what I could tell, the preacher and his Cherokee companions were traveling from the north, so their view of Devil Mountain would have differed from my perspective. But the unwelcome feeling emanating from the place was the same for my brethren back then.

Reverend Cotter went on to scoff at the superstitions of his Native American counterparts, but in the end, he respected their opinion enough to not force the issue of traversing through the 'forbidden' area. Of course, since he was likely greatly outnumbered by his Cherokee companions, pressing through the shadow of Devil Mountain would have meant doing so alone, and in an area often unfriendly to colonists.

"It has got to be the same place," Evelyn advised. "Too many coincidences that your spirit friend would confirm as well. Right?"

"I would say it's the same place, too," I said. "You mentioned that Carmen sent you more information?"

"Would you like to see it? There is some pretty weird shit she included, and frankly I was surprised she sent it along." Evelyn accessed the next file she had downloaded. "Carmen has always been more skeptical than me about certain legends of our people… But then she sent me this, too."

Evelyn opened the file, and at first, I thought she had accessed something incorrectly. The symbols on the screen were Asian.

"This is the stuff I was talking about, which surprised me coming from Carmen," she said. "Have you ever heard of the *jiangshi*?"

I shook my head.

"They're Chinese vampires," said Evelyn. "And they're not just a Chinese myth, as the belief in such creatures is prevalent throughout Asia. Basically, jiangshi are evil spirits that attack human beings and drain their life energy. But there are also actual blood drinking 'gods and goddesses' mentioned in the *Tibetan Book of the Dead.*"

"So, I take it that you must've described what Brigindo looks like to Carmen. Does she now believe you and I are a pair of Native American crack pots?"

"Grandpa, she is one fourth Cherokee. That alone would keep her from dismissing us as a couple of nut cases."

"It hasn't always worked in our favor," I countered. "The less Cherokee presence in the blood, the less trustworthy the person."

"I know you don't mean that, Grandpa!" she scolded, though playfully. "What about David and Miriam? Neither one carries the blood of the Cherokee or any other Native American nation. I can't think of two people I trust more—and I know you feel the same."

True. I would trust David and Miriam with our very lives, and I felt a sudden twinge of guilt for wanting to prevent them from joining us tonight in our return to Blankenship Pines.

"Anyway, there are other examples of vampirism among ancient deities from around the world," she continued. "A consistent theme is that these types of gods and goddesses were born out of sorcery in ancient Egypt and then migrated to different regions throughout the earth. Over time they became distinct from one another, and down through the centuries continued to evolve along different paths."

"So, I guess Brigindo is a confirmed vampire?"

"She fits the bill—as we've already discussed. You saw her, with blood pouring down the front of her body.... And don't forget how Teutates bathed himself in the blood of his victims, too."

How could I ever forget Teutates' behavior? For that matter, how could anyone else?

Evelyn must've been considering the same thing, as she closed her laptop and we moved on to much more positive things—like the day's weather report on TV. Unseasonably low temperatures were in the forecast for the afternoon and evening. We took a moment to discuss how to approach the announcement of what she and I were planning to do that night. Then we waited for the Hobbs clan to awaken, cleansing our palates with a series of *Little House on the Prairie* reruns.

* * * * *

Evelyn's and my planned announcement took a backseat to the unexpected. As tired as we were, the Hobbs family had endured a restless night much worse than ours.

"Oh my God, what happened?"

Evelyn hurried over to Jillian and Chris once they stepped inside our suite. I shared my granddaughter's alarm once I realized both kids had been crying.

"Long story, John and Evelyn," said David, glumly, after he and Miriam followed their children inside, closing and locking the door behind them. "I wish they had got me up when the commotion started."

"What commotion?" I asked.

"The kids heard laughter... and a woman cackling, only worse... like a cat in agony," said Miriam, pulling Jillian close to her. Chris resisted her offer of comfort, but both looked years younger than they had the night before, with red eyes still puffy from a deluge of tears that had only recently subsided. "It happened around five this morning. David and I didn't hear anything, but the kids both said it was loud enough for them to cover their ears."

Evelyn and I were up by then. She and I looked at each other, baffled since both of us had remarked how quiet the hotel seemed.

"It started when Chris came out of the bedroom, since I slept on the sofa last night," Jillian said. "He had a horrible nightmare that seemed so real... *really bad!*"

She couldn't finish telling us what happened, and I feared we might not learn anything about the dream, since Chris shook his head vehemently when Evelyn gently prodded him for details.

"Chris told Miriam he saw Brigindo," David said, finally. "Honestly, if not for what happened afterward I would've assumed it was simply a bad nightmare inspired by what we talked about last night and nothing more. But now I don't know."

He patted his son's shoulder affectionately, and I could see Chris stiffen. I sensed whatever he experienced had left him frightened to the core of his being. But he was determined to appear strong, despite his frayed emotions simmering volatile beneath the façade of coolness.

I wanted to hear about the dream from him directly, as a mixture of his words and the residual images in his mind would provide a clearer picture of what took place and what it possibly meant. Normally I prefer to wait for such details to present themselves naturally, and in due time, since forcing a revelation can lead to important facts being missed. But something prompted me to bypass waiting on Chris or Jill. I instead asked David what he recalled from what Chris told him.

"He wouldn't talk to me... just to Miriam," David replied. He motioned to his wife, who shook her head to indicate she wasn't comfortable repeating what her youngest child had revealed to her. David grimaced. "Sorry, babe, but they need to know what Chris saw in his dream."

"It's okay... honestly," Evelyn assured them both, and turned her attention to Chris. "I might be able to pick up some of what you witnessed on my own, Chris, but hearing it from you would be best."

"I don't want to talk about it," he said sternly, his shy but carefree nature held in check. He again shook his head, glancing nervously at the ceiling as if expecting a repeat performance of what had taken place in his family's suite earlier.

"Apparently, Brigindo was holding Miriam's severed head and mine in her blood-soaked hands while screaming at him in a language he couldn't understand," said David, taking over for his reluctant child. He gently squeezed Chris' shoulder while quietly assuring him and Miriam 'it will be all right'. "Chris told Miriam he was in the woods someplace, and he described an area that sounds a lot like it could be the hills behind Blankenship Pines. A bright blue light was shining through the trees behind her, and he described details about Brigindo that we hadn't shared with either him or Jill."

"The feathers tied at the end of her long braids," said Miriam, quietly.

I honestly had forgotten about the feathers, which was another trait the vile goddess shared with her brother, Teutates. Dark crow feathers were placed throughout his thick black mane. I suddenly remembered that Chris had once seen Teutates in the demon's early state as a hideously withered apparition six years ago, calling him the 'old tree man'. No doubt the most recent vision was as lucid as when Chris, as a youngster, had seen Teutates' specter roaming through the Hobbs' Littleton home.

"After you awoke, you fled your room. Correct?" I asked him, hoping he would provide an answer this time. "How soon after that did you hear the laughter and cackling?"

"It started right after he woke me up," said Jillian, when Chris continued his refusal to talk. "It was really horrible... I have never heard anything like it in my life!"

"Can you remember any of the words?" Evelyn asked her, gently.

"No... I can't. The words sounded weird with harsh consonants... that's all I remember," she said.

Clearly, we weren't going to get much further than this in terms of details. In an effort to improve everyone's outlook, we took a break. I joined Evelyn in whipping up a country breakfast, thankful that she had insisted on doing a little grocery shopping soon after we checked into our suite on Monday. The frightened and haggard looks that had first greeted us morphed into guarded hope.

Once I was confident we had reached the most receptive point we could hope for, I glanced at Evelyn and she nodded approvingly. Then I suggested again—and much more resolutely—for our beloved friends to catch the first flight back to Denver. Miriam and the kids' countenances brightened, while David's fell.

"What? And leave the two of you to fend off these demons by yourselves?" he huffed angrily. "I'm not about to let you do that!"

"My dearest friend... your heart is good and your courage is to be admired," I said, compassionately. "But you and your family remain in danger that will only get worse if you stay here. *All* of us are in danger… but I have a responsibility to take care of this problem, and with no more than Evelyn's assistance. It's not a situation for you or Miriam—and certainly Jill and Chris—to concern yourselves with any longer."

Initially, it didn't go over well. For the next few hours, David sparred heatedly with Evelyn and me, while his family waited anxiously for a final verdict on whether they could go home that day… or not. In the end, a compromise was struck, and David succeeded in delaying a plane ride home to Denver from Asheville by one day. However, it came at the price of him agreeing to stay behind in the hotel until Evelyn and I returned that night from what we also agreed would be our last trip to Blankenship Pines.

Just as David hated the idea of not joining Evelyn and me that evening, Miriam and the kids were less than thrilled with the arrangement to stay one more night. But in their case, having David present helped ease everyone's fears, and staying in our suite seemed to bring additional relief to Chris and Jillian.

"Do you remember the pastes we made for your confrontation with Allie Mae?" Evelyn asked David.

He nodded, smiling weakly. "I guess we're all going to get that sort of protection this time?"

"Yes, exactly," she said. "And, when I pick up the roots and herbs we used before, I'll pick up a few other items to make sure no anisginas can enter either suite."

Miriam volunteered to accompany Evelyn on her mission to locate the proper materials—including horsehair brushes and candles made from beeswax. My granddaughter had remembered to pack her book of incantations, just in case a need for them arose. I suppose we could count that as foresight on her part.

By late afternoon, everything was set, and the suites had been blessed, with all entrances protected. Each of us wore the energized pastes upon our faces, and I smiled at the thought that Galiena might have wanted to add additional ceremonial colors to our faces in the ancient Iroquois tradition... maybe with a touch of the old Gallic too.

To avoid unwanted looks from those curious as to why a party of six wore matching red, white, and black stripes on their faces, we stayed inside and ordered pizza for the second night in a row. Then, once the sun dipped below the mountains to our west, Evelyn and I embraced each of our beloved friends before setting out on the final trek to Devil Mountain....

The time to face a destiny that had burdened my soul from the moment Simon Blankenship first tampered with hallowed ground had finally arrived.

Chapter Thirteen

We expected a host of obstacles to be waiting for us inside Blankenship Pines, but the hindrances began before our arrival.

An especially oppressive feeling embraced us as the Jeep approached the view of Devil Mountain from the highway, as if we had hit a wall of loathing. Evelyn and I were greatly surprised by the phenomenon. The mountain's definition was illuminated just enough by the moon on this cloudless cool night to accentuate its haunting presence.

"Well, at least the weatherman was right this time," I said, hoping to keep things as light as possible.

We anticipated facing real danger of one sort or another within the next twenty minutes. We figured it would be best if it came in the form of homicide detectives or FBI agents still surveying the area for clues to the killings. The confirmed death toll had reached twelve victims after two more mysterious deaths from a few miles away were tied to what had happened at Blankenship Pines. No doubt, these law enforcement officials would be operating with heightened caution and their survival instincts tuned tightly.

But at least these guys would warn us before shooting.

We might not be so lucky if predatory guards similar to the deceased Peter Hundley and Joe Swanson were guarding the development overnight. A bounty on our heads was possible, given Simon Blankenship's disposition toward our people, and toward myself in particular…. But what we mostly expected to face was Brigindo and possibly her siblings—which could be far worse than anything Evelyn had ever witnessed or

138

imagined—including the bloodbath wrought by Teutates in Tennessee that she survived. I know this assumption to be true, based on also surviving that rampage and comparing it to what I had witnessed through Searix's memory. Thankfully, Evelyn had yet to reach that particular hidden alcove in my mind, despite her recent uninvited intrusions into my thoughts.

Galiena's presence stayed with me longer than expected, and in truth it might've remained as a faint essence below the steady increase in my heart rate and accelerated uneasiness. Hard to say for certain amid the threats from Brigindo from the previous afternoon resounding repeatedly in my head, making it almost impossible to focus on anything beyond the task at hand. *Find Brigindo's bones, rebury them in what remains of her ossuary…. Make sure ALL four tombs are secure!*

"The paste on my face and hands is tingling… is it the same for you, Grandpa?" Evelyn asked quietly, once we exited the highway. She looked over at me from the driver's seat, and I could see the mixture of courage and terror in her lovely eyes. Almond-shaped like her sister's and mother's, it was the strongest trait they each had inherited from my late wife, Susanne.

"It is," I confirmed. "The heat tells me that we've already entered the demons' lair."

I hated telling her this almost as much as I disliked not driving—the first step in not having control of our plans that evening. But my night vision isn't so good these days, and saving my eyes from additional strain could spell the difference between life and death once we reached the ravine.

"You remembered to bring the shroud, correct?" I asked.

"Yes, it's folded inside my fanny pack," she said. "I hope it has the effect Miriam thinks it does… maybe it can buy us time if Brigindo attacks."

"What? Are you suggesting that we use it to shoo her away?" I couldn't refrain from chuckling at the mental image of Evelyn whipping the damned thing at Brigindo as if the malevolent goddess were a pesky wasp instead. "And what if it has the opposite effect, and she charges you like an angry bull?"

Evelyn's worried glance at me indicated she hadn't considered that possibility.

"Hopefully we won't need it for anything but wrapping up her bones once we find them," she replied. *"If* we're fortunate enough to make it to the ravine without getting arrested first."

We turned onto the road that would take us to Blankenship Pines. At least compared to our last nocturnal visit, we could see our surroundings fairly well in the moon's glow that was almost a week past its fullness. The pasted stripes on my hands and the one across the bridge of my nose tingled more, and I wondered which of the ingredients among such things as jasmine, chick weed, crows skin, and snake root were most sensitive to the ominous aura emanating from the ravine.

She knows we've come… they all do!

"Look, the gates are open again!"

Evelyn pointed at the welcome invitation in disbelief. I shared her amazement and suspicion.

"Maybe we should park on the street—just in case someone is here… someone human," I said.

"Unless they're hiding, I doubt anyone is here. Definitely no one representing the law is present. Do you see any flashlight beams?" She began to pull in, until I stopped her. "What?"

"Are you forgetting Simon Blankenship's threats against us?" I said, immediately regretting the sternness in my tone. I lowered my voice to shelter my alarm so she would listen with receptive ears and an open mind. "A handful of hired snipers could be waiting in the darkness, ready to pick us off once we get out of the Jeep."

"Really, Grandpa? You can't be serious!" she retorted. "After what happened yesterday, do you really think any rational human being would venture into this place at night and sit around hoping our dumb asses would show up?"

I didn't answer her right away, and I didn't let go of her wrist so she could shift again, either.

"Here we are—the dumb asses—if we take in consideration your comment about rational humans rummaging around here in the darkness," I said seriously. "And, unlike most people, you and I can sense evil on a different level, and see apparitions that others can barely sense. Granted, what lies in wait here is much worse than a typical restless wraith. But my point is this: Some bubba who's fond of coon hunting in these parts might brush aside the fact a few small hairs along the back of his neck are standing up, or pass off footsteps on dry pine needles as merely a deer or rabbit foraging for a nighttime snack."

"Brigindo would tear off Bubba's head before he knew what hit him—"

"True, but only if he didn't suit her purposes," I said, cutting her off as I sensed the danger in lingering where we sat—on the road with the brake lights on. It could draw additional scrutiny if the place was under surveillance by hidden cameras or other means. "You said so yourself that Brigindo sees us as a threat. Might be easiest to have someone shoot us first and ask questions later."

"Okay... so what do you want me to do?"

Good question, since we couldn't sit where we were, and even parking along the main road felt increasingly unwise.

"Pull up just beyond the gates and find a place to park near the temporary guard station. Cut the lights and we should wait a few minutes before venturing any deeper into the neighborhood. It might even be wisest to leave the Jeep near the entrance and travel the rest of the way by foot."

Evelyn eyed me incredulously while shaking her head. Likely, she believed my suggestion was no better than what she had intended to do anyway—although, I envisioned her driving through the development without stopping until she reached the ravine. Maybe she would be more cautious now.

She drove slowly through the entrance and parked facing the roadway's incline as it ascended past the darkened residences that might not get finished for many months to come. Evelyn cut the lights, but resisted my suggestion to cut the engine, too. I didn't push the issue as the hostility in the air around us had steadily intensified since our arrival.

"You might not think I take Blankenship's threats seriously, but damned straight I'm bolting out of here if I even sense a gun being aimed at us," she said. "I'd rather face Brigindo than some asshole toting a rifle—at least my magic has a chance against an unholy spirit."

"We'll soon see about that… hopefully your magic is indeed strong enough, Evelyn." I smiled in the dimness, and she returned it with a smirk—her way of dealing with a situation where she believed the chances of success were unfavorable. I rolled down my window and listened beyond the chorus of crickets and the heavy drone of breath-like cicada calls. I heard the distant chorus of frogs from the ravine, carried downwind in a steady breeze that rustled the treetops. But there was nothing to indicate we had human company. Instead, the air's thickness brought an unsettling ambiance that brought to mind images of whistling through a graveyard. "I don't think anyone else is here among the living… at least I'm not picking up anyone's presence or random thoughts."

"Good. Can we get on with it now?"

"You're the boss once again, my dear."

We shared a moment of quiet laughter that was quickly muted, and she pulled onto the roadway. Ascending toward the ravine, I kept my window rolled down, despite a fall-like chill seeping into the vehicle. Once the ravine came into view, the first thing that stood out to me was the crime scene tape had been moved to where it now blocked all road access moving deeper into the deserted subdivision.

"It must be where they found the guards' severed heads," I said solemnly, after Evelyn repeatedly glanced in that direction as she parked the vehicle. "Hopefully Brigindo's bones are not out there someplace. We should start with the ravine."

"Yes, I agree," she said, her attention increasingly drawn to the hillside beyond the blocked-off area. "She lured them up there. It was to subdue them without anyone spending the night in the house above the ravine hearing a scream…. The family was next. Brigindo likens herself to a lioness, and enjoys the cunningness and sudden surprise of the hunt."

Evelyn carries a stronger clairvoyant gift than what I possess, although I picked up clear images of the demon returning to finish off the terrified men two nights later—as confirmed by Galiena in my dream visitation Monday night. I worried Evelyn might catch details surrounding the guards' deaths that might prove distracting, and I sought to draw her attention back to the present task.

"Can you deliver the incantations with confidence and conviction?"

"Yes, Grandpa…. I memorized the critical portions from the passage we discussed this afternoon," she assured me. "As long as Brigindo doesn't sneak up from behind, we should be in good shape."

"Then it will be my job to make sure that doesn't happen." I gave her what I hoped was a convincing smile.

But like her, I was terrified. We shouldn't be there... and yet if we weren't, I'd never forgive myself if the potential massacre I feared happening in the nearby small communities actually took place.

Evelyn cut the engine but hesitated before opening her door. Certainly, I felt the same thing as she... the weight of an invisible angry stare made it difficult to raise my hand to unlatch my door. My energy was being sapped... until I surrounded myself with white light—something I learned from Two Eagles Cry as a teenager.

"I'm aware, and am blocking it with the same technique, Grandpa," said Evelyn, before I could make the suggestion. "I knew it would be bad, but I didn't expect a spiritual confrontation as much as I did a physical one. Brigindo has already appeared to us in physical form.... Why would she need to hide and attack us from a point unseen?"

"Maybe it's not her," I said. An immediate chill seized my arms and torso, as if confirming this notion. "But we can't remain here for long, and certainly this vehicle won't prevent an assault from reaching us."

Not sure if it was the wisest thing to suggest, since Evelyn's nervousness had become palpable. Surely my own anxiety wasn't helping matters.

"We must be the aggressors here," she said resolutely. "Let's go."

I joined her at the rear of the Jeep, where we grabbed the shovels and flashlights we brought. Then we moved cautiously toward the ravine. Evelyn's attention was again drawn to the hillside she had obsessed about earlier.

"We can take a look up there first if you'd prefer, and then finish our work in the ravine," I suggested. "Maybe that's where Brigindo has hidden her bones. We might stumble on them near an altar, if she's erected one. If so, I'd bet it's where she sacrificed the guards."

Not that I could actually see anything in my mind's eye to support this idea. However, I recalled how Teutates liked to sacrifice his victims, in a bloody altar room located at the top of a tall stone staircase beneath the Cades Cove ravine. Perhaps Brigindo would settle for a steep hillside instead.

Evelyn slowed her pace as if considering revising the plan we had agreed on earlier. She turned her gaze to the hillside once more and then shook her head.

"No... I'm sorry I got distracted, Grandpa. We need to stick with our original plan." She led the way to the ravine. None of it was blocked by tape any longer, and once we stepped around the construction machinery we had a surprisingly clear view of the entire area. "Well... we couldn't have asked for a better night to do this."

Awash in the moon's glow, only the far corners of the ravine were shrouded in shadow. Everything else was illuminated fully—including the gurgling stream that flowed through it. The contrast of clarity as compared to the view of the hillside shrouded in darkness and what the entrance area had been like earlier was remarkable. A new uneasy feeling came over me as I considered how unnaturally dark this place had been during our last nocturnal visit with David and Miriam. Now it was brightly illuminated as if under a noonday sun.

It's too damned easy... like a trap.

Meanwhile, the hostile feeling from earlier increased to where it included an unpleasant sensation of being observed from every angle. Telltale signs that all four entities were aware of our presence and watching our progress....

"Let's not linger," I advised, bravely stepping down into the ravine. "Keep your flashlight handy in case things suddenly go dark on us."

"I was just about to suggest the same thing, Grandpa," Evelyn replied from behind me. "I'm coming!"

Together we crossed the stream and carefully approached the broken ossuary box belonging to Brigindo. It appeared just as we left it the other night, partly submerged in the ground. Even though I knew Brigindo's bones were hidden somewhere else, I peered inside the damaged box. It remained empty.

"Let's make sure the other ossuaries are where they're supposed to be." I paused to survey the ravine while focusing on what Galiena had told me when describing where the other three deities were buried. She had mentioned the tombs were set in the four corners of the ravine, roughly fifty feet away from Brigindo's tomb. "One of them should be over here."

I moved to the northern edge of the ravine's basin. Stepping through thick brush, I ignored the threat of venomous snakes as well as the ever-present animosity in the air around us. Evelyn followed close behind.

"Do you know which one you're looking for?"

"I have no idea which deity the ossuary buried here belongs to," I confessed. "And it may take us a little while to find it… but working together should save some time."

Hopefully, we would locate the portable tomb quickly. It had become impossible to ignore the nerve-racking sense that something unseen was preparing to pounce upon us. Dealing with the supernatural has always been worse than fending off natural threats, as it's maddening to try and guess how or when an assault might happen. A moment of slight relief came when my shovel scraped against the side of something solid. Either a rock, buried root, or the tomb we sought.

"What the hell was that?" whispered Evelyn.

"I don't know... hopefully an ossuary," I replied.

"No... I'm not talking about that," she said, worriedly. She tapped my shoulder and when I looked up she directed my gaze to where one of the graders sat, near the top of the ravine by the parking area. "Something moved from one tree to another over there by the tractor, or whatever the hell that thing is called. See? The branches above it are still swaying from something that was there just a moment ago."

True. Something had recently been there, and a chill along my spine told me it was still somewhere close by... watching us from an invisible vantage point. I tried to rationalize that it was only a squirrel or some other small critter... until I noticed how another branch swayed, as if something fairly strong had pulled upon it for leverage before moving on to the next tree.

"I don't know, Evelyn. It could've been—"

"Shhhh! There it goes again!"

She pointed to another tree, and this one was at least forty feet away from the other two trees... but closer to where we stood. Was it the same invisible presence... or a second one? As with the first instance, whatever had moved the branch remained undetectable.

A sudden snap and thud resounded from a shadowed area not far from where we were digging, in a thick wooded section above the basin. Both of us gasped and whirled to face the spot the noises originated from, flooding it with our flashlight beams. Admittedly, it could've again been something harmless and coincidental in nature, since bigger trees often lose limbs hours after a storm system moves through a forest. Evelyn and I had watched an updated weather report that mentioned the possibility of strong winds affecting the higher elevations in the western side of the state that afternoon and evening.

Yet, if my intuitions were to be trusted, then none of what was taking place had anything to do with the weather.

Something or *someone* wasn't at all happy with our excavation efforts. And, if that perception were correct, in all likelihood we'd soon face bigger interruptions.

"Help me uncover this, Evelyn, before things get crazy."

Casting wary looks around us, we dug furiously to uncover enough of what was buried near our feet. Once we determined it was indeed the ossuary Galiena had mentioned—and thankfully intact—Evelyn sprinkled the remnants of several 'blessed' roots upon the tomb while hastily reciting the incantation she had memorized.

"Do you think it will work like that?" I asked.

"What do you mean… the incantation?"

"Yes. You rushed through the words."

"It's not based on how quickly or slowly you recite the spells, Grandpa!" she replied in irritation. "It's all about the belief and passion behind the words. It's—"

Another creaking branch drew our attention. This one resounded from less than twenty feet ahead of us, toward the southern end of the ravine. A large elm leaned over the basin—not far from where I had watched three now-deceased kids at play less than a week ago. The portion of the tree facing us was plainly visible in the moonlight. A wide trunk and deep ridges in the bark spoke to the tree's longevity, likely a sapling when my grandfather was a young boy.

Much of the elm was healthy, but the rest had been infected by blight. One of the healthier branches from high in the tree suddenly fell to the ground, landing with a loud thud just a few feet away from us. The steepness of the ravine's bank pulled it down and it rolled until it stopped in front of the tip of my shovel held out protectively.

"I think we should go, Evelyn," I whispered, without taking my eyes off the branch. I kept the shovel hovering above it, as if expecting the damned thing to suddenly change into a deadly snake and strike us.

"Grandpa… *Oh my God—look!*"

I raised my gaze to follow Evelyn's, which was locked onto the tree's trunk. When I couldn't detect what she saw, she raised a trembling hand to point it out. Then a pair of camouflaged eyes I hadn't noticed before blinked.

Brigindo is inside the tree? What in the hell?

We watched in terrified amazement as the goddess emerged from the bark's ridges, her solid lavender eyes regarding us coldly. But she grinned mischievously, revealing only a few of her pointed sharp teeth.

Crouching in preparation to launch, her alabaster nakedness glistened cleanly in the moonlight. Stunned by the terrifying realization she'd been observing us from inside the tree's bark the entire time we had been there, I finally shook myself from my stupor and grabbed Evelyn, pushing her toward the ravine's other side to try and make it back to the Jeep.

"Run, Evelyn—don't stop and *don't* look back!" I shouted, not taking my eyes off of Brigindo who stood and took a casual step toward me.

"Grandpa you can't stay here!"

"Just go—I'll be there in a minute!"

The goddess hissed in annoyance as she regarded me. All I had were the pastes upon my face and hands and the shovel for protection, which might prolong my life by a few seconds. Suddenly she disappeared.

I whirled around several times, still expecting an attack. But I couldn't detect her presence anywhere… until I heard Evelyn's voice from above the ravine, chanting in Cherokee. I also heard a louder hiss from our irritated hostess and feared the worst.

Without considering anything beyond her safety, I ran through the stream and clambered up the bank until I reached the parking area. Evelyn was on her knees near one of the graders, with her eyes closed and her hands held palms out above her head. The shroud was laid out before her, and what looked like a swirling mist spun in the air above. My initial thought was she had somehow managed to subdue Brigindo's spiritual essence... until I saw the goddess walking stealthily toward her from behind. My heart prepared me for my beloved granddaughter's execution.

Shit! It's Evelyn's blood they desire... she's the stronger shaman!

"NO!" I shrieked, running toward the demon with the shovel wielded like a spear.

Evelyn turned around to face Brigindo, pulling the shroud with her and bravely waving it at the menacing entity.

"Nihi ase vgalutsv gadohi uyehusv!" she shouted. *You must return to the land of the dead!* Ignoring the swirling mist descending closer from above, Evelyn laid the shroud before her on the ground again while motioning to Brigindo to come closer.

Meanwhile, I had ventured close enough to make out a face within the mist. Dark eyes flashed in anger, while swirls of reddish hair and a long beard obscured much of the face's features. And snakes... there were lots of them!

Smetrios and his vipers? ...He must be close to freedom!

"Evelyn look out!"

But she ignored me, keeping her attention on the deadlier threat creeping up to the edge of the shroud. Evelyn lifted it again. This time Brigindo cackled with glee.

"Nihi uhatia dalasidv ahani!" snarled the goddess in a painfully shrill voice. *You have no authority here!*

I had made it to within a few feet of them. Although she ignored my presence, Brigindo pointed an empty palm in my direction. The shovel flew out of my hands and I was lifted up off my feet and thrown back almost to the ravine, where I landed hard on my back. The blow winded me and I started to lose consciousness…. But, somehow, I managed to roll over and rise to my knees. Nothing was broken… or so I assumed.

Lifting my gaze, I expected to find Evelyn dead with the belief that I'd soon join her. To my surprise, the goddess had backed away from Evelyn, who held the shroud above her head once more. Brigindo circled my granddaughter, as if looking for an open space to strike, and obviously too fearful of grabbing the shroud and tossing it aside. Brigindo hissed angrily when a plaintive whine crept into Smetrios' roars, as if he were helplessly drawn toward the burial garment Evelyn held above her head.

Seeing the war deity's fear of the shroud brought a surge of hope. *He's still vulnerable… he's not like his sister yet!*

His roars became more desperate until they were cut off abruptly. Smetrios' swirling essence began to dissipate—much to the alarm of Brigindo. She seemed to forget our presence, pursuing her brother's lingering misty wisps that were carried by another mountain breeze back toward the ravine.

"Grandpa come on! We might only have a minute to get out of here!"

I was still too weak from the blow to stand on my own. Evelyn helped me to my feet, and despite expecting a third confrontation with Brigindo to happen at any moment, she managed to get me safely to the Jeep. We sped down the drive, as a bloodcurdling shriek of bitter sorrow came to us from the ravine. *Brigindo?* It seemed likely… and in response to the loss of her brother, surely she would thirst for vengeance beyond her normal wickedness.

As we raced back to the highway, Evelyn and I sent repeated prayers to the Great Spirit for protection… and for a huge head start on a vicious entity coming after us all.

Chapter Fourteen

"Maybe she won't follow us."

Evelyn drew my attention from the side mirror, where my gaze had been locked for the past twenty minutes. Fully convinced I would see the white blur of Brigindo coming up fast, I remained tensed in anticipation of the spurned goddess overtaking the Jeep before we made it to the hotel. If the forlorn shriek we heard coming from the ravine meant anything, then making it back to Cherokee without being shoved off the highway would be a divine miracle.

"It's only a matter of time before she comes for us," I said, wishing the heaviness upon my soul would lift. The oppression was the worst I had experienced since losing Susanne more than a decade ago. "We need to work on a plan to protect the Hobbs until morning, and get them to the airport and on a plane to safety. Then…."

"Then what?"

I couldn't honestly say what the next step would be or *should* be. Running from trouble was rarely the wisest choice, unless it meant regrouping and then returning to the battlefield. In our case, the fight was coming to us, and no matter where we retreated to it wouldn't be far enough to escape Brigindo's wrath. It might be wisest to give up the idea of visiting our beloved friends in Colorado for a while, since two thousand miles might not be far enough to evade her reach. The visions of widespread bloodshed due to vengeance forever recorded in Searix's memory thoroughly supported that conclusion.

"Unfortunately, that answer can't be determined yet," I told her. "If only—"

"Galiena could not have reached us back there, Grandpa," interrupted Evelyn, finishing my thought. "Not even my guides could penetrate the wall Abnoba and Abellio created. It was too much for any of them to overcome."

"I thought your guides inspired the dangerous showdown with Brigindo and Smetrios.... You mean that amazing performance was entirely just you?"

I was quite impressed, and at the same time terrified at what might've happened. Something could've easily gone wrong.

"I called upon the only one who wouldn't fail me," she said. "You didn't see him?"

"Whom are you talking about?" I was confused until the answer suddenly occurred to me. "Grandfather? It was *him?*"

"Yes," she said. "Two Eagles Cry appeared to me. At first, I had no idea he was the old warrior standing in the road, dressed in ceremonial beads and full war paint. As you know, we don't have pictures of him since he refused to participate in most 'modern traditions'. He didn't even announce his name until after he and I succeeded in pushing Smetrios to the netherworld beyond the Three Blood Rivers.... He said to tell you that neither he nor Galiena have deserted you. You will soon see this is true."

It was the only time I pulled my gaze away from the mirror on the way back to the hotel. Her words took me aback, as I had indeed been questioning why my grandfather and his preferred 'guide' had abandoned us when the potential crisis we were fighting to stave off was of critical importance.

I had cried to him in silence when I thought Evelyn faced certain death at the hands and teeth of Brigindo. To hear that he actually came to our rescue humbled my heart. I wondered if Galiena had heard me as well, since she remained silent.

"Yes, Grandpa... Two Eagles Cry told me that she also heard you," Evelyn advised, again reading my unprotected thoughts. "This time she was able to come to the ravine, and she kept Abnoba and Abellio occupied long enough to prevent them from attacking either of us with their essences—like what you witnessed Smetrios attempting to do to me."

Evelyn's revelation brought a weak smile to my face... hope was rekindled. Despite another confrontation destined to come, it turned out to be a much better night than what might've been.

We arrived at the hotel just after ten-thirty. The fear and worry had thawed to where we joked lightly about whether or not Chris had saved us a few pizza slices. Evelyn's and my appetites had been almost nonexistent earlier, in anticipation of the upcoming invasion of Blankenship Pines. But now our growling stomachs spoke to the raging hunger no longer subdued, and I pictured a late-night breakfast dinner if the last of the pizza boxes were empty, as I expected.

"Oh shit, Grandpa—*she's here!*"

Evelyn pointed to the eastern edge of the parking lot, less than two hundred feet away from where we parked. We had just removed our gear from the back of the Jeep and had stepped onto the sidewalk that would take us to the breezeway outside our suite. At first, the shimmering figure beneath a street lamp's glow wasn't definable... but once it moved out of a vacant field and onto the asphalt, the hazy form fully materialized. The glowering goddess brushed aside her braided locks that had apparently fallen forward in her effort to catch up to us. But she pursued us with a sauntering gait, as if she had all night to exact her revenge.

"We need to get inside quickly and warn the others, and make sure the doors and windows are still secured!"

Not that Evelyn needed this reminder from me. Already on her way to our suite's entrance, she immediately pounded on the door to get David or Miriam to answer, as if momentarily forgetting she carried a card key to get in. She took mine from me when my hand proved unsteady due to the distraction of monitoring Brigindo's progress.

"Where is she, Grandpa?"

"She's almost to the sidewalk—better get inside now!"

"I'm trying—the damn thing's not working! Where's David and Miriam?"

Suddenly the door opened and the frightened face of Jillian Hobbs peered at us in smeared red, white, and black glory. She looked disoriented amid the blurred pastes that were blended across her face like a toddler's supper. She yawned as if she had been sleeping until a moment ago. No time for an explanation, Evelyn and I pushed our way inside, slamming the door closed when I glimpsed the seven-foot tall goddess in her naked raiment stepping into the breezeway.

"What in the hell's going on?" David asked.

He, too, looked as if he had just awakened, staggering toward where we stood next to the door. Evelyn and I exchanged puzzled looks, and it appeared that Miriam and Chris were crashed out on the sofa and loveseat in the main living area.

"We need to make sure all the windows and the patio door are secure," Evelyn advised. "We don't have much time—"

Something heavy slammed against the front door, invoking images of a medieval battering ram. The door's steel casing stretched toward us until it began to separate. Evelyn's surprised expression turned to terror, and she tentatively approached the door while looking at the top of it, where she had previously arranged several sprigs of dried sage, along with a powder created from several of the roots and herbs she and Miriam purchased that afternoon.

"It's *gone!* Who removed the barrier?"

David and Jillian shook their heads to indicate it wasn't them. Meanwhile, Miriam and Chris had awakened and were sitting up groggily in the living area.

"I'm not believing this shit—you don't remember reaching up and wiping away the boundary?"

Panic had crept into Evelyn's voice as she grabbed Jillian's left wrist, turning it over to reveal residue from the sage and what I recognized as the charcoal appearance of *unaste'tstyu,* or snake roots, from her fingertips to her wristwatch. Jillian looked at her hand in disbelief, as if not recognizing the stains on her skin. She shook her head again… as did David, whose hands looked similar.

Have all the boundaries been compromised?

"It's too late to stop her!" Evelyn lamented, removing her fanny pack and emptying its contents on the dining table, including the small bag of dust she had created from the roots and herbs, along with two bundles of sage sprigs and the shroud. In desperation, she picked up the bag of dust and a sage bundle and moved back to the door, placing them in the door's wound that was now a fist-sized hole.

Long slender fingers, garishly white, reached through the hole and attempted to grasp Evelyn's hand. The fingers withdrew hurriedly after grazing the dust and sprigs.

"Grandpa, come with me—maybe we can slow her down!"

Evelyn didn't need to announce her expectation of finding the windows and sliding patio door similarly compromised. Somehow in their sleeping state the Hobbs had unwittingly disarmed the entire suite. Hard to say when or even how it happened, but I silently rebuked myself for underestimating a group of entities that were of a higher order than anything I had ever encountered this side of Teutates. In addition to the spiritual protection, we had protected against all physical access to the suite. But we failed to account for these unique deities' ability to reach beyond mere obstacles of wood, glass, concrete, and steel—despite the shield of Cherokee magic. Obviously, the pastes and incantations hadn't protected the Hobbs family from being used to tear down the spiritual barriers set in place earlier that evening.

We raced through each room restoring what we could. No longer disoriented, Chris helped David move the heavier furniture in front of the main door that continued to be the focus of Brigindo's initial assault upon our fragile fortress. Miriam and Jillian followed Evelyn's urgings to wipe the dust and snake root residue left on their hands across several windowsills in a desperate attempt to recreate as much of the barriers as possible. Of course, this was largely futile— especially since we were in panic-mode as opposed to our earlier approach delivered with peace and confidence.

"I can't fix everything!" Evelyn reported, when we returned to the main living area. "There isn't enough dust and sprigs to protect two of the windows, and the rest of it needs to be saved for the patio door!"

While preparing what was left for the patio's entrance, a thunderous slam against the suite's main door drew everyone's attention to where David and Chris were fighting to maintain the furniture barricade. The door's frame bore enormous cracks, and the fluorescent glow from the breezeway seeped in through a large fissure near the top. There wasn't an effective way to plug the hole and keep Brigindo out.

"Maybe this could work?"

Miriam held the shroud out to Evelyn while pointing at the hole, soon after I voiced my opinion it might be wisest to retreat into one of the bedrooms. Oddly, at the mention of the shroud, the battering upon the door ceased.

"It might actually do the trick." Evelyn sounded hopeful. "It can't hurt... in fact maybe we should tear off pieces of the shroud and use it on the windows, too."

Desperation often backfires. My gut instinct warned that tearing the shroud into strips, as I envisioned was Evelyn's next intention, might be catastrophic in the long run. What if the damaged shroud no longer worked to bind Brigindo to the spirit realm if we somehow located her bones and could reseal her tomb? Simply sewing it back together might be no more effective than gluing Humpty Dumpty back together.

But my misgivings mattered little in the present moment, as Miriam and Jillian joined Evelyn in a frantic search through the kitchen's drawers for scissors or a sharp knife. The shroud would be torn into pieces within the next minute, and we'd soon learn if this experiment was worth it or not.

Suddenly the curtains to the patio door billowed toward us, as if a windstorm had arrived and the door had been left wide open. Armed with a butcher knife and bone shears, Evelyn and Jillian were preparing to cut the shroud, but stopped and stared helplessly as the seven-foot goddess stepped in through the breach as if the glass door had disappeared. David and Chris moved protectively in front of Miriam and Jillian, armed only with a broken chair leg and a table lamp.

I stood closest to Brigindo. She glared angrily with lips pulled back to reveal her dangerously sharp teeth. I resigned myself to meet her attack head-on in hopes it would allow the others a chance of making it into my bedroom safely. The closer of the two rooms, it was also the one that received the better 'spell repair' job upon the windows.... The shroud might be enough to block the doorway, and from there it would be the

Great Spirit's will to decide if my beloved granddaughter and friends survived.

"Everyone get inside my room *now!*"

Brigindo chuckled meanly, holding me in her gaze through golden braided locks—hair that might be gorgeous on a real woman. Her cold lavender eyes narrowed as she leaned toward me.

"Running Deer... No!" she sneered, venomously. Her voice's shrillness elicited chills in waves that numbed my arms. "They stay... *I feed!*"

I took a brave step forward, ignoring Evelyn's pleas for me to remain where I was, as if this monster was merely a deadly viper or scorpion to be avoided, and not the deliverer of my final moments on Earth. Brigindo's mouth opened wider—like the impossible reconfiguration demonstrated by Teutates long ago. I would die soon. So I intended to send a silent message of love to my granddaughter with another plea for her to make a run for my room.

But just as I expected my life to end, the demon shoved me aside and leapt to where Miriam stood, who was shaking uncontrollably as she held the shroud out before her. I had feared that Evelyn would be the main focus, yet it seemed as if Brigindo had noticed Miriam holding the shroud for the first time. She pushed everyone else away with a mere motion of her hand—very much like what happened to me in the ravine.

"Drop!" the hostile goddess hissed, pointing to the shroud. "Drop, now!"

David fell to his knees begging for Brigindo to take him instead, struggling to no avail against an invisible force that kept him from getting any closer to Miriam. Surely recognizing his current plight from what he had experienced years ago from both Allie Mae McCormick and Teutates, in desperation he pleaded for his beloved wife to cooperate, ignoring the pointlessness of negotiating with a remorseless demon. I mourned the fact it would be Miriam initially appeasing Brigindo's appetite, rather than me.

"Running Deer... it doesn't have to end this way!"

Galiena... you're actually here?

I dared not speak in the faint hope Brigindo wasn't aware of my guide's presence. For the moment, Miriam remained the focus, shrinking to her knees before the goddess and holding the shroud above her face as if a child again and attempting to hide under bedcovers from a boogeyman. Her grip on tenuous sanity might finally crack this time.

"How can it possibly end differently?" I asked silently.

"Watch and wait," Galiena advised, suddenly materializing next to me. Her appearance was disheveled, and the war paint she favored was streaked from tears. Her struggle to protect us from Abnoba and Abellio in the ravine, as reported by Evelyn, must've been incredibly intense. "Now's not the time to explain, Running Deer. *Listen!* Miriam's spirit is telling her to cling to the shroud... the spirit knows what it is. When Brigindo moves in to smite Miriam, tell her to throw the shroud at the goddess. It's the only way this will work in your favor."

"Can't you see that Miriam is too terrified to do anything? Brigindo has already won the battle!"

"Then you shall also lose and we can continue this discussion from my side of the veil," she said, evenly. "Tell her to throw the shroud Running Deer... tell her *now!*"

At that very moment, Brigindo's anger at Miriam's refusal to cooperate—and in all likelihood too terrified to even think coherently—escalated, and the demon's jaws opened wide enough to engulf Miriam's head. Things would turn horrific in the next few seconds.

"Throw the shroud at her, Miriam!" I shouted. *"Do it now!"*

Only Evelyn seemed to understand the implied meaning behind my words, and she echoed my urging with a heartrending shriek. David and Chris looked on helplessly, unable to free themselves from invisible shackles that easily subdued them.

Brigindo closed her jaws and Miriam ducked away at the last instant. Still, it appeared she would continue to cling to the shroud, until she suddenly pushed it toward the entity's head. Brigindo pulled her head out of the way and the shroud landed on her right shoulder. Immediately, the flesh fell away from the shoulder down to the monster's menacing fingernails. The bones we had sought unsuccessfully at Blankenship Pines fell to the floor.

She hid her bones within herself? Shit—how obvious, and yet so different from how her brother Teutates hid his skeleton....

Brilliant and yet foolhardy, since carrying her bones left the entity vulnerable to attack. Enraged, Brigindo resumed her intent to devour Miriam. But in that instant, her hold on the rest of us ended.

"David, push her away!" I yelled.

Brigindo, leered at me over her shoulder, but without her arm she would have to turn and face me in order to use the other. The fingernails in her left hand suddenly morphed into raptor-like talons—surely deadly enough to take each of us down in a single fell swoop.

But David and Chris distracted her long enough for me to grab the shroud that had drifted toward me. I grabbed it and leapt at her while holding the burial cloth out in front of me, stretching my arms to their limit. Keep in mind this wasn't an Olympic athlete crashing into her torso, but a 'seventy-three-years-young' former park ranger expecting to be dispatched into the afterlife.

The moment the shroud touched her body, the flesh disintegrated again. This time, it didn't stop until I had placed the shroud over every exposed area of Brigindo's shrinking form. All that remained in the end was her head, which fell to the floor and rolled toward Miriam, who desperately scooted away. When the head stopped rolling, Brigindo's eyes regarded me narrowly, and her mouth moved to speak…. But before she could utter some sort of curse or dying threat, I covered her head in the shroud.

Her hair detached first followed by her deadly jawbone dislodging from the skull. While David moved to comfort Miriam with their children, a raspy sigh of my name escaped from beneath the shroud. The last sound was of the goddess' teeth falling out of the sockets and rolling on the hardwood floor out of view.

A night manager and policemen were pounding on the front door, calling to Evelyn and me. We would have to answer… there were damages to pay for, too. But the wicked goddess of the ancient Gauls had been defeated. Her bones lay haphazardly upon the living room floor, covered in the dust that moments earlier had been her vibrantly unholy flesh.

Despite the uncomfortable questions soon to come, and answers that might not make sense to anyone unaware of just how close we had come to further mayhem in this region, the hard part was over… finally.

Chapter Fifteen

By the time the night manager and policeman were able to enter our suite, Evelyn and David had wrapped Brigindo's remains inside the shroud. Bones, I might add, that were in a petrified state as Galiena had previously asserted they would be. It magnified the horrific illusion of how the goddess had incorporated them into her physical presence.

Brigindo had appeared as real as any other 'flesh and blood' creature, when in fact she was a dead thing preying on the living—a vampire in every sense of the word, despite the term being reserved for monsters of fantasy and ancient folklore. We had witnessed the miracle of an existence that defied natural laws, if not reason. But it was no less real, given the trail of death Brigindo had left in her wake.

I shuddered at the thought of how much worse things could've become, amid a modern world that surely would've been slow to understand her nature and intentions, as well as those of her siblings. Keep in mind the rampage of Teutates had largely been forgotten in Tennessee. The federal government swooped into Blount and Sevier counties right after his brief reign of terror, and quickly transformed the growing legend of a living demon into a faceless serial killer dispatched in the subsequent destruction of Teutates' temple—a structure altered in the news reports to be an abandoned cabin in the Smokies' forgotten wilderness.

As far as anyone presently knew—outside of those who survived Teutates' attacks—there was no enraged deity back then, wreaking havoc from Cades Cove to Knoxville.

Certainly, in our present circumstances it would be that way again.

Evelyn and I understood before we ventured to North Carolina that without our brethren's help, we would have no choice but to publicly downplay what was happening in Blankenship Pines. The local authorities would scoff at tales of ancient Gallic gods and goddesses aroused from their millennium-long slumber to slaughter the locals, and the feds would seek to shut us up... likely by use of deadly force if necessary.

When one Sevierville deputy mysteriously disappeared following an interview with a news station in Knoxville, not long after Teutates' murderous campaign ended, Evelyn and I knew from then on we must keep the details of what happened a secret. If not for this written account, and what escaped the authorities' censor in two books about the events of Cades Cove that Evelyn discovered online last year, no one would be the wiser. Even to this day, my buddy Butch Silva—who was the Sevierville Sheriff at the time—refuses to acknowledge what happened in Cades Cove. Surely the local cops in Cherokee would end up following similar protocol.... So why waste a single breath telling the truth? Because when given in small doses to make us all look crazy, there might be safety in insanity....

"Tell us what happened to the door?" asked Ahsan Khan, the night manager.

He stood at the edge of the living area, keeping a respectful distance from the six of us seated on the sofa and loveseat. Jeremy Weathers, an officer with the city's police department sat behind him at the dining table. The officer surveyed the entire living and kitchen areas while conversing in code via his radio with a dispatcher. So far neither man had noticed a missing chair out of four that had originally surrounded the table, as that one lay broken and buried in one of the bedroom closets beneath a spare blanket. As for the door in question… it had since fallen off its hinges when Chris and I finally got it open. The only reason we didn't advise our visitors to come around back to the porch for easier access to the suite was to allow everyone else more time to straighten things up as much as possible.

Mr. Khan and Officer Weathers waited for a response with wary eyes, most likely due to our disheveled appearance as a group. I thanked the Great Spirit that Miriam had enough presence of mind to enlist Jillian's help in washing the pastes from our faces and hands. Only small traces of the snake root's residue remained visible. Heaven knows what the two men would've thought had our faces looked like our beleaguered Sioux brothers and sisters at Wounded Knee.

"I wish we knew," I replied, after glancing at my granddaughter and our friends. None of them knew where to begin, and I was the one best suited for skirting the details with half-truths. Honesty is the best policy unless the truth is impossible to believe. "Something slammed into the door, and when it couldn't get in here, it turned violent… like a grizzly."

"Are you saying a bear or some other wild animal did this?" Officer Weathers shook his head in disbelief, while Mr. Khan's eyes grew wide. It didn't matter that grizzly bears lived more than two thousand miles away in the Rocky Mountain region of the country. Khan looked at the splintered door, obviously picturing something along the lines of a giant menacing bear tearing through the door's steel casing.

"Not necessarily… but it was something angry and powerful enough to cause us to fear for our lives," I said, maintaining the role as our spokesperson. Since the suite was rented in my name, I assumed any damage and possible criminal penalties would be leveled against me anyway. "What took you so long to show up?"

My question brought a surprised look from the night manager and an admiring grin from Evelyn.

"Several guests down the hall reported the noise," said Khan, whose condescending stance from a moment ago had taken on an 'oh shit!' quality, and it was almost entertaining to discern the change of words scrolling through his head, moving from such terms as *jail time* and *commendation* to *lawsuit* and *getting fired.* "I called the police immediately, since we were concerned for everyone's safety."

Good answer, Mr. Night Manager.

"I'm surprised more people didn't hear the commotion," I continued. "We expected someone to come to our rescue much sooner."

"Why didn't y'all call the front desk or police yourselves?" asked Officer Weathers, his focus directed mostly at me, though he had taken an interest in Evelyn.

"Because, like what my grandfather's trying to explain, we were frightened and fighting to stay alive," she interjected. "Do you think any rational person really would've had the presence of mind to call *anyone* while whatever damaged the door was about to come inside? Especially, if we were placed on hold by some overworked dispatcher!"

I would've thought her response was too harsh, but the sudden embarrassed look on the policeman's face spoke to recognition. Evelyn quite likely had lifted the dispatcher information from Officer Weather's thoughts.

Our combined efforts as a group proved to be the difference between getting hauled off to jail for disturbing the peace, and having Mr. Khan arrange a move to two suites on the opposite end of the property at no additional cost to us. We didn't get settled until shortly after midnight, and as before, Evelyn and I shared one suite and the Hobbs stayed in the other. Despite the new 'clean' location we hardly slept that night. None of us felt comfortable having Brigindo's bones nearby, but we would've worried more had they been kept anywhere else. So, I kept them near where I lay.

"Carmen should be up by now," Evelyn announced shortly after five o'clock that morning. I was finishing the brew for a fresh pot of coffee. "Hopefully she can place an emergency call to Dr. Hewitt, to get him to come back to North Carolina a day early."

"Why do we need his help?" I followed her into the living room. She was already dialing Carmen's cell number. "I thought you and I would return to the ravine and rebury Brigindo's remains alone. You said the other three anisginas are safely contained, so what more can Dr. Hewitt do for us?"

"Grandpa, let me take care of this and then I'll explain," she said, turning away when Carmen answered.

I decided to wait at the dining table, paging through a courtesy copy of the latest *USA Today* left under our front door sometime in the last hour. I tried to ignore the conversation going on nearby, allowing only Evelyn's upbeat tone to filter through my attention to the newspaper's headlines.

"So, I take it your conversation went well?"

I motioned for her to join me at the table when she finished speaking with Dr. Rainwater. Evelyn poured herself a cup of coffee first and then sat down, smiling proudly.

"Yes. Carmen got a hold of Dr. Hewitt last night, while we were exploring the ravine," she said. "He's very interested in helping us and should be back in North Carolina this morning. She asked if we could stop by her office around three o'clock this afternoon. She's expecting him around two-thirty, which will give him a chance to rest before examining Brigindo's skeleton."

"Why does he need to examine the bones?" I asked, admittedly leery of him touching anything that was safely protected by the shroud. Hell, I didn't want to unwrap the damned thing ever again, as I worried it might give Brigindo a new invitation to return to our world.

"Grandpa... it's what he does for a living," said Evelyn, pausing to sip her coffee. "And, I hear your worry about the risks.... We need him fully on board to not only get the bones reburied, but also to stop Simon Blankenship permanently."

Evelyn went on to explain that Carmen had called her yesterday, expressing at that time what it might take to get enough help to shut down Blankenship Pines forever. We already knew Dr. Hewitt would carry some influence due to his tenure and position at UNC. However, he apparently was also well connected with the North Carolina legislature.

If we could impress him with the unusual attributes of the skeleton—such as the age, size, and predatory aspects such as the unusual teeth—the ravine and the surrounding areas would forever be protected from plunder by law.

But there remained the problem of reburial of the bones, and keeping the other three ossuaries from being unearthed. Those were my big sticking points.

"Well, it's the main downside to this arrangement," she admitted. "But according to Carmen, Dr. Hewitt is better suited than anyone else she knows—including anyone associated with the reservation—to protect all four tombs and the area they were discovered in from being further exploited. Still, I share your worry that something could go awry while the professor and his team of assistants unearths the ossuaries to take photographs and accurate measurements."

"I don't like that idea," I said, feeling a chill cross my heart. "Something could get lost if the bones are transferred to the University for additional study and cataloging before the final interment takes place—like what happened to Teutates' bones in Tennessee. Even something as small as a finger bone could provide these entities—these dangerous predators—a new foothold in our world. Do you not remember what I told you about the true origin of the Bell Witch?"

"You mean how the young Bell boys took a small fragment of a bone from the ancient burial mounds on a bluff overlooking the Red River?"

"Yes. Believed to be a finger bone, it fell through the floorboards in the old Bell Cabin, and the spirit began its hostile attacks soon after," I said. "How much worse would it be if one of Brigindo's bones becomes lost in transit to North Carolina University?"

It became the question I thought about most while waiting to meet with Dr. Hewitt. Meanwhile, once David, Miriam and the kids knocked on our door just before eight o'clock, Evelyn and I again urged them to return to Colorado that day. As I expected, despite being exhausted physically and spiritually, they weren't about to leave us until they knew for certain we'd be okay.

They say true friends will die for another. I believe this is truly how it is for the Hobbs and us. However, it is better to strive to live rather than remain in harm's way. So, I resolved to make sure we had spent our last night in Cherokee, and before the sun faded in the west that evening, we would be on our way back to Tennessee. Even so, I prayed our departure would be with a resolution in North Carolina I could live with.

Carmen Rainwater was waiting for us when we arrived at her office that afternoon. Dr. Peter Hewitt stood by her side, and looked taller than I expected, although the graying goatee and bushy brown hair with intense blue eyes were what I had foreseen through my mind's eye. He had brought a large steel case to house the remains. At least he came prepared.

Galiena had appeared to me during our short road trip from Cherokee. Speaking from the Jeep's backseat, she advised not to cling to my suspicions of Dr. Hewitt, as well as my worries pertaining to the fate of Brigindo and her siblings.

"You must let it go, Running Deer…. Brigindo is now too frail to rise again," she assured me. "Two Eagles Cry succeeded in pushing Abellio and Abnoba beyond the Three Blood Rivers, where Smetrios also now resides. Brigindo is weakened by their absence and will find it difficult to regain her ability to manifest fully."

"So, what happens if this professor fails to come through with a permanent solution? What if Blankenship wins in court, despite all the deaths that took place on his property?" I asked quietly, to which Evelyn responded with a curious glance until she realized I wasn't talking to her and returned her attention to the road ahead.

And, as had become her habit, Galiena vanished again without a reply….

"Carmen has told me a lot about you both," Dr. Hewitt said, after shaking Evelyn's and my hands. He smiled warmly while greeting David and Miriam, too, and offered a lighthearted joke to Jillian about changing her mind and coming to UNC for her college education instead of Denver University.

"Are those the bones?" Carmen asked, pointing at the duffel bag I carried which contained Brigindo's remains still wrapped in the shroud.

"Yes," I replied, feeling a sudden heaviness descend upon the office. I could tell Carmen felt something too, as she wrapped her arms around herself, as if a chill much cooler than the air conditioning had suddenly seized her.

Galiena…. Grandfather…. If either of you can hear me, please stay close, and bind the others from finding their way back here.

Evelyn's smile to the professor and Hobbs' kids defied the worry in her eyes. She felt it too. Brigindo was near... perhaps watching with curiosity as to what would transpire with her remains.

"Great... let's have a look at them in the boardroom," said Carmen.

We followed her and the professor to the glassed-in room. He playfully referred to it as 'Carmen's fishbowl', to which she responded with a nervous laugh. Fortunately, the lawyers and accountants sharing the building with Ms. Rainwater were absent at present. Having to explain the presence of what likely would appear to be a deformed human skeleton spread out on the boardroom table would only increase the possibility of something unfortunate happening, and seemed most unwise.

Concerned about even the slightest bone dust escaping the shroud's protection, I enlisted Evelyn, Miriam, and David to help me carefully uncover the bones after I gently lifted the burial cloth out of the duffel and placed it in the center of the long cherry table.

"Oh my God!" gasped Jillian.

Chris shared her surprised reaction, as they both pointed at the skull and detached jawbone. Although none of us had looked at the bones since placing them inside the duffel, Chris and Jillian had recovered two of the loose teeth that had fallen out of the shroud when David and I lifted it from the hardwood floor in our former suite. Most of the teeth were left in a small pile in the midst of the other bones... but now they had somehow found their way into each empty socket. Both the skull and jawbone looked especially menacing with twin rows of sharp pointed teeth.

"Well, this is really something," whispered Dr. Hewitt, reverently. He moved up to the skull, carefully lifting it and bringing it close to his eyes for a better view. All the while I fought the urge to tell him to set the damned thing down before he hurt himself. I could tell Evelyn was holding her breath until he completed the same process with the jawbone. "I have never seen something like this in person... just in photographs."

"Really? So, this isn't something that's one of a kind?"

David sounded disappointed. Meanwhile, the professor's effusive warmth from moments ago had given way to an air of seriousness. I sensed the change wasn't inspired by fear. Rather it was fascination. My misgivings were heightened about handing the bones over to him... but the look on Evelyn's face told me to hold off interfering.

"On the contrary, it's quite rare," he said. "This is the only specimen I've seen or even heard of in North America. The previous skeletons were discovered in Bosnia, not far from the pyramids everyone likes to crack jokes about. But there are only pictures now, as those bones were stolen a few years ago.... There are some differences, and if Carmen hadn't told me about your version of how they found their way to North America over a thousand years ago, I would be inclined to believe this skeleton was a stolen artifact that somehow made it into the United States during modern times."

"Even with the fact until a week ago, it was buried in Blankenship Pines, which sits below the place known to the Cherokee as *Tsvsgina Odalv?*" I found myself getting angry. I understood there were other remains—likely many more than what he suggested, and surely scattered throughout the world. The legends of ancient gods and goddesses were many.

"Devil Mountain? Yes, I know of the place and its storied past," he said, unfazed by my simmering indignation. "Carmen and I have discussed everything you've shared with her at length, along with what she has uncovered on her own. Mr. Running Deer, I can assure you that I have no intention of letting these remains fall into the wrong hands, and my commitment to you is the same one I expressed to Carmen before your arrival. After the standard tests and cataloging are completed, we will see to it that not only this specimen will be returned to the tomb in Blankenship Pines, but the others buried there now will also be restored and protected."

He paused to look at Carmen, who nodded to confirm the truth of his words. Evelyn responded in kind, though not as fervently, indicating she carried some doubt. I saw the split soul before me, as I sensed Dr. Hewitt would try to do the right thing... but he wasn't beyond influence. I doubted he held a single conviction that couldn't be overturned at the right price.

"I have some very influential friends on Capitol Hill," he said. "And I have friends in Washington, too.... If necessary, I will either get Simon Blankenship's ownership rights revoked, or in the very least keep him from digging anywhere near the ravine. There is precedent for putting a barrier or fence around the ravine's perimeter to protect the tombs from being harmed in any way. As much as I might be tempted to turn something like this over to the protection of the Smithsonian, I am sensitive to the beliefs of your people even more. I can thank my friendship with Carmen for that." He laughed... it sounded forced.

"So, you promise to rebury this skeleton and allow a shaman from the reservation here, or the one in Oklahoma, to perform the traditional ceremony to ensure all four tombs are properly sealed and blessed?" Evelyn asked. I sensed the desperation... she was ready to let go of the responsibility. In truth, who wanted to baby sit something as evil and with the potential to create widespread bloodshed? It suddenly occurred to me that maybe Galiena no longer wanted to be a babysitter, and her request for help was also a plea for escape.

I began to feel helpless, about to be pulled wherever the popular current favored.

"Yes," he said evenly. "I swear it upon my very life."

A serious oath beyond what the professor understood, or so I believed. But it would have to be good enough, despite the expressions on each of the Hobbs' faces reflecting my own doubt. They had seen the same things Evelyn and I witnessed, from a living goddess on a rampage to Brigindo's seeming departure from our world; and now in this fancy room, the evidence the goddess had returned long enough to fix her dental work.

Maybe the solution needed to be out of our hands. Were the old ways of handling such things with magic and the wisdom of spirit guides from the other side of the veil destined to give way to new 'modern' insights based on pragmatism and science? And would Dr. Hewitt remain sensitive to our beliefs and customs when he returned Brigindo's remains to the ravine as promised—hopefully with a court order's blessing to tear down the log mansions of Blankenship Pines?

These questions stayed in the forefront of my mind as I watched the professor carefully add the bones to foam compartments inside the steel case he brought. And the same concerns returned to me later, as Evelyn and I headed back to Tennessee with David Hobbs matching my granddaughter's lead-foot on the gas pedal.

There was so little we could control. The fate of Brigindo, her siblings, and the safety of all things lying in the shadow of Devil Mountain were no longer up to us.

Chapter Sixteen

The trip back to Tennessee was largely uneventful, other than Evelyn getting pulled over for speeding. My granddaughter can be stubborn and doesn't always heed her premonitions—especially when inconvenient to do so.

"At least it didn't happen while we were out of state," she quipped, after David and I teased her about it, once we made it back safe and sound to my cabin in Sevier county. "I'll get it expunged from my record by taking the 'safe driver' course online."

"But will you remember to listen to the 'still small voice' inside you next time?" I said, drawing a rolled eye response. "Better yet, will you listen to your grandfather's warnings? There's more than one shaman in this family, you know."

"Oh, so you finally confess that it's your calling?" she shot back playfully.

"I was referring to Shawn."

Since our beloved husky was just as glad to be home after we stopped to pick him up from Butch's place on the way back, my comment drew a brief wave of laughter. It helped launch a jovial mood that brought the cathartic relief we all needed badly after dealing with so much death and danger during the past week.

When we left Carmen's office, David and Miriam had already made tentative plans to change their flight back to Denver to the following day, instead of next week as originally scheduled. However, by the next morning, Friday, they put off leaving until after the weekend. Yet, regardless of how well the

Hobbs were recovering from our North Carolina misadventure, Evelyn and I knew that they'd need a few days to decompress from it all in their Littleton home, before having to get back into their normal routines.

Without the immediate worry of what might happen in North Carolina, along with no signs that anything unwanted had followed us back to Tennessee, the weekend turned out to be the vacation we and our dear friends had hoped for when we hammered out the plans for the visit to Gatlinburg this past April. All the activities we had been forced to miss while dealing with Brigindo and her brief reign of terror were back on the menu. Surprisingly, we managed to do most of them… hiking, fishing, horseback riding, and even a return to Dollywood in nearby Pigeon Forge. At night, after hitting the arcades and go-cart tracks for the kids and visiting Miriam's and David's favorite restaurants along the famed Gatlinburg strip, we returned to the hot tub with the wonderful view from the Hobbs' rented chalet.

Sunday night, David refused Evelyn's and my offer to share the cost, since they missed several days at the pricey venue perched above the town. He also advised this would be the last time he would have anything 'willingly' to do with the supernatural.

"I'm getting too old for this shit," he said, out of earshot of Miriam and the kids.

"Really? Last time I checked, *I'm* the card-carrying AARP member here!"

My joke brought a chuckle from Evelyn, but only a pained look from my dear friend.

"I'm serious, John," he said. "I thought I could still handle everything just fine. But I felt like I was going to have a heart attack out there a few times, man…. I'm going to get in better health, and one thing I think will help is staying the hell away from ghosts, demons—or whatever creatures Teutates and Brigindo are. I've spent way too long thinking about Allie Mae, the damned ravine, Norm…. so many things."

In truth, Evelyn and I had worried about his health as well. Years of inactivity due to long hours working to grow his CPA business had left him in less than optimal shape physically— especially when dealing with powerful entities that would give no quarter for his condition. However, I should've also considered the lingering toll the events from long ago had on him. Miriam obviously wasn't the only one to suffer lasting effects from their shared encounter with Teutates. David carried the additional scars from having to deal directly with the ghost of Allie Mae McCormick, who murdered David's best friend, Norman Sowell.

"We all would do well to avoid such creatures, David," I said, compassionately. "For Evelyn and me it might not be possible, since whatever power governs the universe has seen fit to bless—or curse—us with the ability to discern such entities. But we will do whatever we can to keep you and your family safe from such things going forward…. Does this mean you would prefer we not come to see you and Miriam in the fall?"

"Oh, hell, no—I still want you to come! Miriam is already planning fun things for us to do, and we'll have the guest rooms ready for you both," he assured us, smiling sheepishly as if he wished he had worded his denouncement more diplomatically. "And, I'm really looking forward to your visit, too…. Just don't bring Allie Mae and her buddies along with you."

We shared a better laugh and he returned to his family gathered on the back deck, enjoying the pleasant night air and the view of downtown Gatlinburg below. A peaceful feeling washed over me as I watched them, and I believed full healing would come to them all. Perhaps it might be better to quietly exit the Hobbs' lives in order to ensure their lasting happiness.

"They might need us again someday," whispered Evelyn, standing beside me.

"You don't think it would be better if we backed off a bit?"

"Grandpa, we see them once or twice a year—tops," she said, rebuking me lightheartedly. "Backing out of their lives isn't at all what they need or even want. David is dealing with a little post-traumatic stress. You—his best friend now that Norm's long gone—need to remain active in his life. Just be ghost-less." She lovingly massaged my shoulder, and I clasped her hand.

"I believe you're the wisest person I know, dear granddaughter," I told her, gently squeezing her fingers. It was what I needed to hear.

We rejoined them, and our last night together was one destined to be among the most memorable. Not because of any significant event, but rather the feeling of camaraderie confirmed our enduring mutual love and respect for one another. It made it easier to say goodbye the following afternoon after an enthusiastic affirmation by Evelyn and me to come see them on their turf in just a few months.

"I'm already wishing it was September... or October, if that's when my fall break comes," Evelyn advised, once we returned to the cabin. "I'll have to check my class schedule."

"A trip to Colorado is something I'm looking forward to as well," I said. We stood together on the deck facing the rear of my property. Shawn was taking care of his personal business, and a feeling of peace emanated toward me from the forest beyond my property line. It grew stronger as it drew my focus.

Galiena? It's good to feel you, my friend....

She didn't respond by appearing or answering my unspoken thought. But the feeling of contentment continued to enwrap my entire being… until a vision suddenly fell upon me, like an unexpected glass of ice water thrown into my face. My connection to the blissful moment was lost.

As such things often go, my spirit was swiftly transported somewhere else… this time to an unfamiliar building, similar in style to the campus structures in Knoxville. But I recognized other landmarks that told me the vision was coming from Chapel Hill in North Carolina.

The air was crisp and cool, and the leaves had begun to turn. Soon a sea of orange, yellow, and purple would engulf the famed city and university. Students dressed in early fall attire walked around me, sharing jokes about their classes and calling to one another jovially as if I wasn't there. From the conversations of a few kids, I determined a big game was happening that weekend, although I couldn't pick up who was coming to town to play the Tar Heels. That information might come in handy in determining when another event—the one I was drawn to—would take place.

As touched upon above, I wasn't physically present at Chapel Hill. Nor would I be, since I didn't detect my presence in normal reality—which has happened with some visions that involve those I care about. But my spirit had been called here for a reason… something ominous was coming. Something that my soul told me I couldn't prevent, but needed to see nonetheless….

"You know, Grandpa… we might be called back someday to Cherokee, and we need to be ready for when that happens."

Evelyn's words jolted me, pulling part of my awareness back to the present while the vision continued to engage my mind and spirit.

"You think so, huh?" I tried to sound evasive, longing for the blissful state that had faded, like the warmth on a winter day when the sun's rays disappear behind a cloud.

My mind was pulled like a magnet to a specific event not yet played out in our reality…. I had somehow entered the building—a marvelous structure erected not long after the university was founded at the end of the eighteenth century. I had moved up to the top floor, largely deserted, although my footsteps were silent upon the two-hundred-year-old heart pine floors.

Things moved more quickly from there, and I found myself inside a large room and standing in front of a long wooden table bearing the bones of Brigindo. They were spread out, and some had paper labels attached to them, while others did not. Dr. Hewitt sat at a desk not far from the table, but with his back turned toward it. I peered over his shoulder, and saw that he was entering details about the bones into a journal—a process Evelyn and I had hoped would be completed long before the school year started, and truly should've been a top priority when he left Dr. Rainwater's office on July 9th.

Suddenly, my attention was drawn to the table, and before my eyes the bones began to assemble themselves while taking on the flesh and alabaster qualities of a bloodthirsty goddess— one who had killed thousands of people in her long existence on Earth. She regarded me curiously with her cold lavender eyes, but said nothing, her smirk showing her amusement and contempt.

Obviously, I was a mere phantom to her—a ghost in her reality. Without making a sound, she stepped down from the table and moved past me in predatory silence. The professor must've sensed her stealthy approach, as I noticed a wave of fine hairs standing on end along his neckline. He casually turned his head to see what his protective instincts had alerted him about.

All I was allowed to witness was the professor's horrified expression, and the bloodcurdling scream as my spirit rapidly returned to where I stood on the deck....

"Yes, I do," said Evelyn, nodding while wearing a puzzled look. I tried to hide as much of the vision as I could, though I could feel her worriedly scanning my head for clues about why I had gone from a peaceful demeanor to one of uneasiness. I could tell I was frowning, but couldn't force a smile bright enough to hide the truth of what I felt. "Or, you and I might be called into action to help someone else... maybe in another part of the country."

"What, to some place like Idaho or Kansas?" I teased. Actually, either location sounded like a vacation compared to going back to North Carolina... at least as long as Brigindo held sway over the land.

"Maybe... or perhaps it will be a bunch of places spread out all across America," she replied, returning my playful jab with her own. Her smile was returning, although she couldn't hide her concern. "I get the feeling you're not keen on venturing forth to help those in need. What's up?"

Her words cut my heart, since I have always sought to help those in need. That outlook is what got us in this pickle to begin with, since I wouldn't let David Hobbs perish at the hands of a spirit determined to kill him. I knew in my heart that Allie Mae McCormick could complete the task she intended, unless someone with the insights of Evelyn or me stepped in to help.

"I just don't think I'll be up for it, Evy," I said, ready to dismiss the idea and move on to something else. "I think I should consider retirement from everything but my garden... and maybe a good book now and then, and my favorite shows on TV."

"Are you sure?" An impish light flickered in her eyes. "Because that's not what she's telling me."

"Whom are you referring to?"

"Her."

Evelyn pointed to the tree line where the earlier warm feeling had come from. Galiena stood in the shade of the tall pines with her arms folded across her chest. Once she caught my attention, she smiled and waved at me and stepped into the sunlight, where her essence dissipated.

"Galiena says you and I have much work still to do, and not just here," said Evelyn. "There are many anisginas wreaking havoc throughout the world, and she says we've been called to help those in crisis here in the States. Not just in Tennessee and North Carolina. Like me, she's looking forward to a reprieve from guarding the ravine, and has offered to come along with us."

Greatly surprised by this revelation, it took me a moment to gather my thoughts and respond

"Let me get this straight…. Galiena spoke to you… you're now friends… and she wants to be our manager in all things spiritual?"

"Yep!"

"Hmmm." I needed time to process the vision I had just been given, and other than planning to contact Dr. Hewitt and encourage him to fulfill his promise to diligently rebury Brigindo's bones, I honestly wasn't in a hurry to go chasing after spirits of any kind. I couldn't commit one way or another until I had time to let the proposition and all ramifications sink in. But at least I was no longer the only one who could see my enigmatic spirit guide. "We'll just have to see about that, won't we? I have melons and squash that will be ready for harvesting soon…. Besides, don't you have school and a boyfriend to tend to?"

"Jeff can wait," she said. "Besides, when he's off on one of his business trips, I can help you save the world from itself. And as far as school is concerned, when everything started getting crazy earlier this week, I contacted Dr. Forsyth. I asked him about handling most of what's left in my master's program online. He said it shouldn't be a problem at all!"

Evelyn's excitement was contagious. Maybe getting away from worrying about events we couldn't control would be a good thing.

"Well, we'll see…. Hopefully there isn't much 'saving the world' that needs to be done," I said, gazing toward the spot where Galiena had disappeared. "I'd prefer facing something more benign next time."

Despite my reluctance, I realized all I had been doing for the past six years was putting off the inevitable. Evelyn was right… I could feel the call to my soul to not withhold spiritual rescue assistance from those who needed it.

So what's next? I suppose it depends on where the strongest pull comes from, and when the forces that own the night bring trouble and heartache to the innocent. If the Great Spirit is willing, my ornery granddaughter and I will be there… along with our evasive guide and friend, Galiena.

Peace to you all,

John

Devil Mountain

The End

~~~~~~~~~~~~~~~

About the Author

Aiden James is the bestselling author of *Cades Cove*, *The Judas Chronicles*, and *Nick Caine Adventures* (with J.R. Rain). The author has published over thirty books and resides in Tennessee with his wife, Fiona, and an ornery little dog named Pepper.

To learn more, please visit AidenJamesNovelist.com, or look for him on Facebook (Aiden James, Paranormal Adventure Author) and on Twitter (@AidenJames3).

Made in the USA
Columbia, SC
28 November 2021

49902365R00107